But A Wandering Voice

By M. L. Tapper

K-Nurse, Book 2

Sousa House Press
Montpelier, Vermont 05602

This book is a work of fiction. All characters, names, places, and events are a product of the author's imagination or are used fictitiously. Any resemblance to persons living or dead, companies or events is entirely coincidental.

ISBN: 978-0-9989066-5-2

Cover design by Marianne Nowicki

O blithe New-comer! I have heard,
I hear thee and rejoice.
O Cuckoo! shall I call thee Bird,
Or but a wandering Voice?

"To the Cuckoo"
William Wordsworth

For Arthur and Felix

One

Château de Vincennes, Paris, April 1940.

Augustine, resplendent in a bleached and starched white apron and headscarf, sat down on the wooden bench next to me and handed me a cup of soup. I sipped it loudly while we sat in silence, both staring ahead at the foggy window. A rime of ice had formed on the inside of the ancient leaded glass, thickening each day with the breath of hundreds of French officers.

The château was the headquarters of General Maurice Gamelin, commander in chief of French forces, and the epicenter of French military defense. Men in camel hair coats with all manner of decorations filed by us in both directions, their kepis under their left arms, polished boots reflecting the light.

"Jude says Gamelin is smart and measured and that we have superior numbers," Augustine said.

"Superior numbers don't mean as much with modern weapons," I replied. "One guy with a machine gun is worth five hundred with swords, or muskets, for that matter."

Augustine nodded.

1

"Jude isn't doing any nurse work anymore," she said. "He caught Gamelin's eye somehow and got a promotion to capitaine. He's in the general's inner circle, or at least the outside of the inner circle."

"The outer circle," I said.

Augustine sighed.

"Either way," I said, smiling, "we've got somebody on the inside. If the Returned have an agent there, Jude can hunt them down."

"Them?" Augustine asked.

"Could be a man or a woman. Could be more than one," I said.

"Definitely a man," Augustine said, frowning. "I have yet to find any woman above the rank of *sous-lieutenant*. My boss has told me I'll never be more than an *aspirant*," she said, referencing an officer rank that wasn't quite an officer at all.

"A man, then," I conceded. "If there's an agent, Jude will find him."

"Our brother is a relentless hunter," she agreed.

Simon slid onto the bench next to Augustine.

"Where's my soup?" he asked.

"Didn't know you were going to be here," Augustine replied, and a look passed between them. *That* kind of look. Those two had been off-again, on-again since the Napoleonic Wars. Which reminded me of something.

"Didn't Gamelin's father or grandfather or something fight with Napoleon?" I asked.

"At Solferino," Simon replied. "Jude says the general never shuts up about it. He finds a way to work it into conversation whenever he can."

"Those were heady times," Augustine said wistfully.

"So, what's the news from the north?" I asked Simon, purposefully breaking whatever romantic spell was brewing.

"The bigwigs are saying there's just no way for the Germans to get into France. The terrain in the Ardennes is too difficult to cross and the Maginot Line is impenetrable."

"Impenetrable. How many times have we heard that?" Augustine mused.

"You gotta admit it's a pretty impressive bulwark," I said.

"They always are," Augustine added.

"The rumors, though, are troubling," said Simon. "One of the orderlies I know was drinking with one of the air force mechanics who said their pilots spotted a long line of German trucks at the German border with Luxembourg. I mean a *long* line, maybe two hundred kilometers. The pilots were excited when they landed. They figured we had the Germans dead-to-rights, but the brass just shrugged it off."

We sat in silence for a while. I had no more soup to slurp.

"Last week," Simon continued, "the pilots said the Germans were building bridges on the Our river."

"Sounds like the Germans think France is impossible to invade," I said. "They're planning to go around, just like the general predicted." I looked at my watch and slapped my thighs before rising. "I've got a shift in a few minutes."

"I'm sorry you can't be on the floor with us," Augustine said.

Men were not nurses in the early twentieth century, only women. That left most of the K-Nurses with few good options. Peter and Thomas had made the sacrifice of becoming physicians. It wasn't that close to nursing, but they would have to make do. Jamie was an engineer, and Simon and I were orderlies, but we would be mustered out as medics if real fighting started. Bart ran the motor pool in Sedan, up on the Belgium border, and Phil was training on the new D.520 fighter.

For now, it was bedpans, brooms, and breakfast; we, the humble night shift, served the *petit déjeuner*.

All ten knights were in this world. All were assigned to the Allied forces, and for the last two months the air had been pent with approaching darkness, really since Hitler had invaded Poland. We worked, we kept in touch as we could, and we held our breath.

France and the Reich exhaled on May 9, and all hell broke loose.

Bart was killed in the German offensive across the Meuse river, and Philip was shot down by the Luftwaffe three days later. Two weeks after that, Simon and I were in Calais with the sea at our backs surrounded by Germans. The carnage was the worst either of us had seen, and, in our nine hundred years, we had seen some genocide-level invasions. The hospital was overrun, and men bled to death on the battlements around the city. We were running out of bullets and shells on the third day of the siege.

I was awoken in the night by a hooded figure who motioned toward their mouth with one finger to indicate silence. I swung my MAS-36 carbine until it was level with the hood. But I did it very quietly. The figure held both hands up and flipped their hood back.

I couldn't tell whether it was a man or a woman, the face was so badly scarred from burning. Their eyes were barely lidded. Their ears just coiled stumps. A thin line of drool trailed out of the hole that had once been a mouth.

The figure looked at me with urgent eyes, and I followed them as they retreated out of the barracks, down winding stairways, and finally to a tunnel that sloped down to the water. The figure pointed into the mouth of the tunnel. I lit a match, and they slapped it from my hand to sizzled on the wet ground. No light, then.

Placing my hand flat against the smooth wall on the left side of the tunnel, I slid my feet forward a few centimeters at a time, my eyes growing accustomed to the dark enough to see reflected starlight at the far end. A dinghy waited just beyond the tunnel mouth. Simon was already inside, lying over the bow to make his silhouette smaller and to be able to hoist the anchor quickly and silently. Behind him, hands on the oars, was Peter, our leader since the twelfth century. He was wearing an Adrian helmet, standard issue for the infantry. I always thought it looked like the head of a penis. Seeing it on Peter made me chuckle, and I had to cover my mouth. I slipped over the side and into the boat and lay down in the middle, while the anchor chain clinked softly against the gunwale, then the splash of the oars. The sounds of German artillery and small arms fire faded as we paddled away.

My body warmed and dried in the bottom of the dinghy, which told me that we were under a cloaking spell and that Peter was seeing to my comfort. Maybe not such a penis after all. By the time we arrived at Dover, a thick fog had fallen, concealing our approach. Peter led us to a cave in the cliffs where a fire burned in a pit of stones. Jude, in full dress uniform, was shackled to one wall of the cave, while the remaining Knight-Nurses of the Order of St. John, K-Nurses for short, huddled near the fire. Thomas sat nearest Jude with his eyes closed, no doubt maintaining the binding spell.

"You know I'm right," Jude shouted, but the sound diminished as if by the turn of a volume knob.

"What's he right about?" I asked, unbuttoning my jacket. Now that I was toasty and dry, the fire was too much for me.

"He says the Nazis are the future. That they will bring order and stop the mindless cruelty of the modern world," said Augustine.

"I'd hate to think we chain up a brother for having misguided political opinions," I said, looking at Jude who was apparently screaming, his mouth frothing. No sound came from him.

"He was the Returned spy in French command," Peter said.

I couldn't, I wouldn't believe that. Jude and I had fought side by side for centuries. We had both died caring for victims of the plague. I had seen him sacrifice so much for the innocent and the suffering. He was my brother.

"I don't buy it," Simon said, as if reading my mind. "There must be some mistake."

"As did we all," Peter replied. He looked old as the cliffs around us. He had not had a new incarnation in four centuries, using his magic to be our institutional memory and leader, and he looked every day of it. "I would not have called this tribunal unless the proof was unassailable. You're right, Paul, he is our brother. Doing this feels like cutting off my own hand."

Jude thrashed at his bonds.

"I have seen the workings of his mind," Thomas murmured, and we all turned to him. Thomas was the best user of magic in our order. Ordinarily, it would be a breach of trust to enter another knight's consciousness. It would also have been damn near impossible, since we were all well trained in defense against such psychic attacks. When Thomas used his power to its fullest, though, he was scary powerful.

"He was too distracted to keep me out," Thomas said. "And his handlers don't have much magical power in this world." Thomas opened his palm, and a little movie appeared above it. Two Returned executives, Gamaliel, vice president of Human Resources, and Thagirion, corporate counsel, stood on either side of Jude weaving darkness around him. The image of Jude in Thomas's hand spoke so quietly it sounded like buzzing. Thomas made a sign with his other hand and the voice rose until we could all hear him.

"They don't understand now," Jude said. "But they will. The knights are wise, trust me on this. The Nazis will finally bring order to this world, finally whip the chaos into something beautiful. My brothers and sister will see this, just give them time." The static rose again. I think it was the Returned speaking, but Thomas said nothing about it. When the sound resolved again, Jude's betrayal was clear.

"General Gamelin will do anything I tell him to do, and I have told him to ignore the intelligence on Wehrmacht movement into the Ardennes. You will have the French on their backs before they realize their mistake."

Although he could not speak, Jude must have heard all of this, because at this last part, he slumped into his bonds and closed his eyes.

A fat tear rolled down Simon's cheek. James wrapped his arms around his knees and rocked. Peter turned his back to us, his hunched shoulders shuddering. Augustine, stone-faced, surveyed the room. She straightened, and her hair stood on end as her whole body began to glow. Thomas, also glowing, reached out to hold her hand. Then Simon and Peter joined the circle. Then James came, and finally, I opened myself to whatever it is that releases the power inside me and completed the circle.

We glowed like a captured star, and Thomas spoke, his voice a cacophony of all our voices.

"You have betrayed us, Jude. You have given comfort to our enemies and brought suffering to those we must always protect. Ibn Jamay raised you and imbued you with our returning life. Not even we can kill you. Your punishment is banishment. With our power in this circle, we banish you to the Ether for four hundred years. You reap the bitter harvest you have sown. You will answer when we call. You will serve us against our enemy in penance. Be gone. Seek forgiveness. Only with the greatest suffering can you atone."

A great roar, like a train passing through the cave, heralded a spinning wind that sucked the light from us. The blinding tornado spun away, engulfing Jude, whose screams were short and heartbreaking.

Then the light went out. The cave was silent, and Jude was gone.

Two

Election Night, Part One

And there was Jude joking with a reporter. The lights caught his perfectly white teeth and shirt. His blue suit shimmered slightly, sparkles reflecting from silver cuff links. He raised his head to look at a display behind him and pumped his fist when he saw that Pennsylvania had been called for Garridan Roosevelt.

I passed the bowl of popcorn to James, who was sitting on the couch next to Augustine, his legs drawn up under his chin. He put a handful of popcorn in his mouth, then passed it to Augustine without ever moving his eyes from the TV.

"He played us for such fools," he said. "I still can't believe it."

"The power behind the throne," Peter chimed in from the kitchen.

"Don't be so sure," Thomas added. "Remember who Garridan Roosevelt is. He's so heavily warded, I can't even tell if he's using magic on the election."

"Or how many more of them are here in our world now," Augustine said.

"No, I can't tell that either," Thomas replied. He coughed into his elbow, a dry, wracking sound that made all of us turn. He waved us all away before he had even stopped coughing. "Just a chip stuck in my throat, be cool," he said. "We need a plan for each contingency, if he wins, if he doesn't. His people are so strung out, anything could happen if he loses."

"We have to get out of here first," said Simon.

One of the Returned might become president of the United States, and we were imprisoned in our own wards, nothing in or out.

"We also need options if they break in," Augustine said. We all knew her well enough to know she was scared, even if she gave no indication. "That's for after the election, though. They wouldn't do anything tonight. They'll be too busy either celebrating or running amok for a coordinated attack on us."

"The betrayer tries to frighten us," Peter said. "We must not give him the satisfaction of responding in desperation."

"He's been ahead of us during the whole campaign," Augustine replied without turning. "And now he thinks he's got us at each other's throats."

Ohio was called for Roosevelt.

The name Roosevelt was sure to incite even more division in this divided country. Roosevelt. Teddy was the great narcissist and individualist. Franklin was the steward of such socialism as there was in this country. Garridan was way to the right of Teddy, but he would invoke the New Deal whenever he felt he could get some applause. He constantly implied that both Teddy and Franklin were his forebears, choosing between them as suited the crowd in front of him. Garridan loved applause. Sometimes his speeches were like an open-mike stand-up act. Lots of bad double entendres with a sly wink to the audience, as if to say, "This is just between us girls."

No presidential candidate had been so openly and unapologetically racist since the 1950s. When confronted about it, Roosevelt laughed and said he was the least racist person who had ever run for public office. Up is down, black is white.

His rise in the polls was as puzzling as it was dramatic. He had no experience at all in the public sector. He had been known as a gadfly in Prentiss Gilchrist's orbit. Gilchrist was the Returned executive that Aurora had dispatched on her first mission. After Gilchrist's assassination, Roosevelt sold himself as the natural successor. He was already well-placed in Gilchrist's network as one of his biggest donors. His billions had opened a lot of doors and bought a lot of support. In the end, it had worked. The same anger, intolerance, and ignorance that had been lifting Gilchrist was now a tsunami under Roosevelt.

Peter's front door creaked open and shut, and I heard two loud, wet kisses, one on each cheek, before Aurora came into the room and plopped down on the arm of my chair.

"'Sup, Pops?" she said.

I raised an eyebrow and looked up at her. She looked soulfully into my eyes. We had so many unspoken tensions.

"Did you have lunch?" I asked.

"Two days in a row. Can you believe it? And I've planned for a snack while we watch."

I patted her arm.

"I'm relieved to hear it."

11

Our steady string of losses throughout the last three months had taken a toll on Aurora's "sobriety." She had entrusted Augustine to keep her honest, and now Augustine kept track of all of Aurora's food and exercise. Aurora's battle with anorexia would last her whole life. I hoped that if she was reborn, it would not follow her, but there was no sure way to know. We weren't even sure she would be reincarnated like the rest of us.

"Any report from in town?" Augustine called from the couch.

"There's a crowd forming in front of Penn Center," James said, referring to a community center just up the road from our headquarters.

"That's not weird on election night," I said. "People have been gathering there forever to watch the election results."

"Yeah," James said, "except it's all white people."

"At Penn Center?" Thomas asked. St. Helena Island, where Penn Center was built, was ninety percent Black.

"Not a person of color anywhere out there," James explained. "It looks like a rally for Roosevelt." Peter passed a tray of charcuterie around before setting it down on the long table behind the couch. There were smoked meats, cheeses, pâté, and terrine. Peter made country terrine to die for.

His house, Amalfi, where we were watching the election results, was sparsely decorated, but each piece of furniture, each figurine or statue, every painting, was a masterpiece. His wine cellar would have made a Master Sommelier weep. Peter had brandy from the Napoleonic Wars that was no doubt undrinkable, but fantastically valuable. Nevertheless, he couldn't bring himself to sell it. Miguel, our former squire, had lived at Amalfi House in Peter's spare bedroom after we rescued him from the

Left Hand of God. He had been like a son to Peter before the possession.

Florida was called for Garridan Roosevelt, and the room groaned as one.

Peter pushed an easy chair over to the couch, and picking up a slice of baguette and salami, he chewed, looking at each of us in turn.

"We should consider permanently moving our headquarters," he said when he had swallowed the little sandwich. "It's too dangerous here. They know where to find us."

"I disagree, chief," Thomas said. "This is where the Returned are going to make their play. There's no better place to make our stand."

"If Roosevelt wins, I guess that's midnight on the Big Clock," I said, and I saw Augustine shudder.

The Returned's greatest desire was to bring their whole company (the center of their world) across the dimensional gateway. Their dimension, the Ether, was a two-dimensional place. It was as gray as a Vladivostok housing development. Everyone and everything worshipped the almighty company. At the highest levels of company management were the Returned, ten of them to mirror the ten Knight-Nurses of the Order of St. John. No more than ten could come into our world at any time. Unless.

We didn't know how they had originally opened the gateway to our world, but we knew that there was a specific kind of energy involved, the loathsome energy that ruled their world, that kept the population under the Returned's bootheel. Thomas had theorized that if the Returned could cultivate enough of that energy in our world, they could let their hordes flood through. This evil energy was generated by cronyism, race hatred, religious intolerance, subjugation of people on the basis of gender, or age, or any one of a thousand arbitrary categories. If they could create enough of that kind of thinking in our world, it would bring our destruction.

We kept track of it on a doomsday clock. When that clock struck midnight, the world as we knew it would be overrun. We were at about five minutes to midnight, by Thomas's reckoning on election night. He and James had the ability to sense this tide. Although their measure of the Returned's influence was magic and not science, Thomas wasn't usually wrong in his predictions, and James had enough foresight to fill in any gaps in Thomas's visions.

Michigan was called for Roosevelt, and that put him over the number of electoral votes he needed to win. Garridan Roosevelt would be the next president.

The screen showed celebration at Roosevelt's election headquarters. Jude, his campaign manager and a former knight, pumped his fist in the air. Time stopped for me, as though I was on the liminal edge of waking from a dream. None of the disasters I had witnessed through history was as surprising as this.

Popping sounds in the distance pushed me back to the present. These were sounds I would have taken for fireworks at another time, but which were much more sinister now. A bright, loud flash erupted in front of headquarters, sending glowing green ripples over the shell protecting us. Someone was firing magic ordnance against our wards.

The lights went out. I could *feel* the wards failing. It was like the end of a battle when you took off your armor and watched it fall to the ground, so exhausted that it was as though you watched it from a great distance. You were suddenly cool and exposed.

In front of our previously invisible headquarters, the illusion of dense vegetation melted away. Crackling gunfire and breaking glass made us all drop to the floor. Peter pressed a button on the TV remote, and a section of the tiled floor slid out of the way. Red emergency lights flickered in the opening. One by one, we crawled to it and ran down the stairs.

I had just taken an American-made AK-47 from the rack in the basement and levered in a magazine, when the room above, the room I had just left, became a tunnel of fire.

Part One: July, Four Months Before the Election

Three

I pulled the rental car under a twenty-foot-high arch made of hemlock logs, the entryway to a Lander, Wyoming hot spot restaurant, the kind of thing you would expect in an old cowboy movie—*This here's the Flyin' V Ranch!*—and parked in the row across from the front door. Aurora and Miranda were waiting for me by the entrance.

"Ladies," I said, making a little bow.

"Evening, kind sir," Miranda replied, curtsying with an imaginary skirt. She was in blue jeans and cowboy boots. Aurora hid her smile behind her fist, which was in front of her mouth to cover an obviously fake cough.

"You guys done?" she asked, then threw her arms around me. "It's nice up here in the mountains."

"It is beautiful," I conceded, "but a touch too rural for my tastes. The health center is pretty small."

"The Medical Center in Casper is awesome. I'm working on a

stepdown unit," she said, taking my hand and Miranda's hand and pulling us toward the big double doors. She dragged us right up to the maître d's station.

"Party of three," Miranda said. The host smiled at me, but I caught him glancing at Aurora's and Miranda's hands. It was just a second, but it was obvious just the same.

We sat at a long bench facing the fancy western bar, complete with polished rails and a mirror behind the liquor shelves.

"How was the drive?" I asked.

Aurora tilted her head.

"How's the weather up here, Pop?" she replied.

"So, no small talk, then," I said.

Miranda leaned forward, conspiratorially.

"We made good time," she said, and that got all of us laughing.

Our waitress, Charlene, was small, with close-cropped jet-black hair. She wore cowboy boots of many bright colors and a gray Stetson. She took in Aurora and Miranda and a half-smile crept up her face.

"Well, howdy hi and how are y'all?" she said too loudly. I must have jumped a little, because she twisted toward me and lowered her head. "Sorry, buddy, gotta keep up the patter for the rubes." This time her accent was pure New Jersey.

"I understand" was all I could manage after a couple of blinks.

"Can I get y'all somethin' to whet yer whistle?" she said in her big-as-all-outdoors voice.

"Can I get a seltzer with a slice of lime," Miranda replied in a sizzling vocal fry (look it up) reminding me at that moment that she was in fact from *the* valley. She was playing it up, but she did it so deadpan no one who didn't know her would have guessed. Aurora snorted.

"Sure thing, toots," Charlene said. "I'm gonna have to see some ID, though." She stuck out her arm like a chicken wing as if to poke Miranda in the ribs. "Just joshin' ya." An older man in a western hat, an honest-to-god ten-gallon hat, tipped the brim to us as he, uh, sidled up to our table.

"Evenin' folks," he said. "Charlene here'll take good care of you. You just let me know if you need anything a'tall."

Charlene watched him disappear into the kitchen. Her whole posture relaxed. "How about you, miss?" she said to Aurora in a way that made it absolutely clear that she was flirting.

"Watch it," said Miranda, and this time there was no Valley Girl in her voice."

Charlene cocked her head and put her hands on her hips.

"Easy does it, girly," she said very quietly. "It's hard for a queer girl here in West Bumfuck."

"Gin and tonic," Aurora said, breaking the tension and smiling at Charlene. I saw the muscles on one arm flex and guessed that she was squeezing Miranda's hand.

"Scotch for me," I added.

"Coming right up," New Jersey Charlene said. She walked past the bartender on her way to the kitchen. He reached down and patted her behind. She spun on him.

"How many fucking times I gotta tell you, Jerry. Knock it the fuck off."

She was squared off with Jerry now, he a full head taller. He laughed, which made her grind her teeth so hard we could see her jaw flexing from across the room. The kitchen door swung open, and the manager made a beeline for Charlene.

"That is no way for a lady to speak," the manager said.

"Allowing this dickhead to slap my ass whenever he wants is no way to treat a lady either, but here we are, Bud."

Bud looked to the ceiling.

"Give me your apron, Charlene, you're done," Bud said.

She untied the apron and threw it at him.

"Happy fucking trails, you, you shit-kicking loser," Charlene hissed before marching out of the dining room, her festive boots clomping loudly on the linoleum floor. The two men looked at each other, knowing smiles crossing their faces, as if they were in on a secret together.

"Jesus, what an asshole," Miranda whispered.

"It's enough to make you want to turn in your penis," I agreed.

"Ew," said Aurora. "Could we please not reference your penis during dinner, or, for that matter, ever, under any circumstances, until the end of time, amen?"

"Have you ever been a woman, Paul?" Miranda asked, as if it was the most natural question in the world.

"I haven't," I admitted. "Always a man. Some of the other K-Nurses have come back as women, though."

"What?!" Aurora cried. "Why am I just hearing about this now?"

"I didn't know you were interested," I said. "You knew about Augustine."

"Yes, yes, I knew about Augustine," she said, making a rolling motion with her hands.

"Andrew has had several female incarnations," I said.

"That's the shrink," Aurora muttered to Miranda.

"Oh," she murmured back, but never took her eyes off me.

"Simon was a woman during the French Revolution, and he hated it *so* much. Luckily, he hasn't been a woman again. At least not yet."

"Seventeen hundreds, yeah, that must have sucked," Miranda said.

"Peter has only had about six lives, but two of them were as women," I said.

"He's hundreds of years old," Aurora said to Miranda, this time cutting her eyes in Miranda's direction.

I know it was childish.

I just stopped talking and sat there staring at Aurora, who narrowed her eyes.

"Well," she said. "What about Thomas?"

21

"I'm sorry. Is it my turn to speak? I didn't want to interrupt."

Miranda's eyes went wide.

"Oh, snap," she said. "I hope they bring the drinks soon. You're going to need some ice for that burn."

Aurora sighed.

"You were saying, before you were so rudely interrupted?" Aurora said, her voice flat. She ignored Miranda.

"Yes, well, Thomas is like me, always born as a male," I replied. "He's not happy about it. He has all kinds of theories about how it could affect his power, in a good way. And he really likes men, sexually. He wants to know what it would be like to experience sex with a man as a woman."

"Way too much information," Aurora said. "That's my brother-in-arms you're talking about. He'd like to try out being a woman, that's all you had to say."

"Hmm," Miranda said. "That leaves James."

"Right," I replied. "James is asexual, has been since the beginning. He's usually born pretty androgynous, and his birth sex isn't always the gender he goes by. I don't have James's permission to tell you much more than that."

"What if he grows a beard?" Miranda asked.

"It just looks like old lady chin hairs. I've been on surveillance with him and that's how it looks after a couple of days without shaving," Aurora said.

The bartender arrived with our drinks. Miranda pushed hers back to him.

"I said lime," she said, staring directly at him. "This is lemon."

"Well now, little lady—" he began.

"Take it back and bring me seltzer with lime. And don't you ever 'little lady' me."

"Well now, hold on, ma'am."

I had lost my patience.

"Bring her the drink she ordered, *now*," I said, slapping my open hand on the table.

"Yes, sir," he replied, scooping up the glass.

As soon as he was gone, Aurora rounded on me.

"Don't do that," she spat. "We don't need a man to fight our battles for us."

"Of course you don't," I said. And damn it, I knew she was right as soon as she said it. "This place is stressing me out."

"Me, too," Miranda said, putting her hand on mine.

I looked at Aurora smugly. Miranda understood me. Aurora squinted, her battle face dropping into place.

I excused myself to go to the men's room. I wasn't running away. It was more of a tactical retreat.

When I got back, both women were bent over their phones. The food had appeared in front of each place, and the air was taut.

Bon appétit!

"I'm sorry," I said, lifting my sandwich for a bite.

Aurora looked up and frowned.

"Let's not make a federal case out of it. Just don't be such a douchebag next time." She crunched a potato chip as if she were mashing bone.

"Speaking of federal cases," Miranda began, scowling at Aurora, "the FBI has raided a troll farm right here in the US. The report says there's a network of these all-over North America, but they, the Americans, don't have jurisdiction in Canada or Mexico, so they're relying on 'interagency cooperation.' Whatever that means. But in Canada, really? Imagine a troll farm up in the Yukon or, like, a bunker in the Arctic somewhere, just spewing out shit on social media. It's ridiculous."

I could imagine it. I was imagining it right that second, and it seemed like a great way to hide your nefarious activities: go where there were no people. It could have been the desert or the jungle, but somehow, the tundra made more sense.

"Out of the mouth of babes," Aurora said, raising her eyebrows up and down. "The smoking-hot kind. This hadn't even occurred to me until you said it. I think social media trolls, and I think big city. Putting it out somewhere, well, somewhere like the arctic would make a lot of sense. Good OPSEC."

"Operational security," I explained to Miranda.

"Smoking hot, huh?" Miranda said, ignoring me. She leaned her forehead to touch Aurora's.

Dear lord.

"I, too, think that's an inspired idea," I said, hoping I didn't blush. "I'll ask James to see what he can find. If he does locate a troll farm, Aurora, are you ready to go break some tech?"

"I was born ready to break shit," Aurora answered.

"She really was," Miranda purred.

Dear lord.

Four

Seven kilometers east-southeast of Stein Fiord, Nunavut.

The wheels on our plane groaned as we slid to a stop on a high plateau
north of the Arctic Circle. Our landing area was ringed by mountains in
every direction except to the west, where a long, shallow lake sluiced
into a break in the ridge. It being summer, the temperature was a balmy
four degrees (about forty degrees Fahrenheit), and a constant mountain
wind blew from the north toward the ocean.

We inflated the Zodiac and paddled the three kilometers across the
bracing lake. It was *bracing*, not cold AF, mind you, for we are Knights
of the Order of St. John. We spit in the eye of the elements. It was
bracing, like a brisk walk in outer space. We set up a landing area east of
the town.

Village? Settlement? All is context.

Whatever it was called, it was a cluster of squat buildings along the

26

shore. Grim does not even begin to describe it. I admit, I've got plenty of aesthetic prejudices. I used to think a wet, drafty castle was nice. Maybe the folks here love it. It is beautiful in the way the desert is beautiful, the way a hungry tiger is beautiful.

We came in over a stony ridge southeast of the town's little airport. It never gets dark in July this far north, so we had to rely on magical camouflage once we topped the mountain overlooking the town. The brown, stony trails were completely exposed and would have made us sitting ducks without the magic. James maintained the spell while he tried to pick up transmissions from below. We stopped while he adjusted equipment, opened his computer, and took out his binoculars, all while nodding to himself.

He motioned for us to look at the screen.

"There's a rough dirt road, rougher than the other rough dirt roads here, that leads up the mountain north of the reservoir. They have a satellite dish out there. I saw it from our satellite image, but it must be north of the ridge, so we can't see it from here. Right along the southern face of that ridgeline is a door. There are gun emplacements all around it."

"They're guarding a door into the side of a mountain out *here*?" Simon's face was covered by a scarf and goggles. He hates the cold. His question barely made it through all the woolen layers.

"That's how I knew they were here," James replied. "The guns and the dish."

"Any other way in?" Aurora asked.

"Not that I can see," James replied.

"Diversion?" That was Andrew, the psych nurse, always thinking of the mind games.

"I dunno," James said. "They've put surveillance cameras around the bowl leading up to that door."

This line of ridges, like waves in the ocean, was made of different stratified layers of rock. I sent my consciousness down into it. Even minerals, or rather, their atoms and molecules, have a peculiar kind of awareness. They don't think, but they bend, in a strange way, around experience. I found the stratum that extended under the guarded doorway.

"We can flow through the rock," I said, becoming aware again of my surroundings.

"We can't take the weapons, though," Simon said.

"We could," James interrupted, "but it would cost us a lot. We don't need another knight in the hospital."

"Thomas could use the company," I remarked. Our main mage was in the hospital with uncontrolled hypertension.

On the whole, we like smart aleckry. This time, nothing but crickets. You can't win them all. They all looked at me for an agonizing second, then turned to James's screen without comment.

"If we flow into the center, it's all hand-to-hand," James continued. "And we don't know how many are in there."

"We have the element of surprise," said Andrew.

"True," James admitted, "but that will only take us so far. It won't help much against forty or fifty guards."

Aurora stripped off her coat and tactical vest, unbuckled the belt with her sidearm and knives. Then she pulled her sweater over her head.

"Whoa!" said Andrew, covering his eyes.

James turned at the sound to see Aurora unbuttoning her bra.

"Yikes!" he squeaked and pulled his hood over his face.

I put my back to her.

"Reconnaissance?" I called over my shoulder.

"Yeah," she said, followed by the sound of her thick pants hitting the rock. There was the kind of whooshing sound that accompanies projection magic and then a tapping of rubber on rock. I turned around to see Aurora's boots upside down on the rocks, flapping. She had forgotten to take them off before flowing into the rock. I undid the laces and pulled them off. Her milk-white feet slid into the rock and were gone.

We waited. James monitored his screen, which became a swirl of unfocused pixels, then resolved. In the distance there was a loud pop, like a .22 shot into a metal barrel. A bramble patch of black hair emerged from the rock, and we all spun away from it. Aurora made the groaning, grunting sounds of someone who has just gotten out of an ice-cold pond and is rushing to get all their clothes back on.

"It's safe," she said, teeth chattering.

Andrew placed his hand on the rock we squatted on, and it became warm. Aurora's eyes crossed with relief.

"What happened in there?" James asked when Aurora had stopped shivering.

"It was a huge server farm with lots of pasty boys and girls at computers. No guards or anything inside, although I could feel serious magic all around the outside of the structure."

"But none underneath," I said.

Aurora shot me with her thumb and index finger and nodded.

"Where did she learn that?" Simon asked, not even trying to hide his annoyance.

"Shucks," I said with a deadpan.

Simon looked away first, grumbling.

"Alright," James said, unslinging his pack. We all stood up and began shedding our gear.

"Hold up there," Aurora said. "Where are you going?"

"To destroy the troll farm," I said. I flipped the slide on my nine millimeter, catching the ejected round while I dropped the magazine into a pocket in my vest.

"It's done," she said.

We all turned.

"I put a little extra juice into their power mains and fried everything. They were all crashing into each other in the dark when I flowed out of there."

We were silent. Andrew opened and closed his mouth several times. James just smiled.

"Booyah," Simon murmured. He held out his fist, which Aurora bumped. They both opened their hands at the touch as if their fists were exploding. Simon tilted his head at me.

"Booyah. Absolutely," I said, and refastened the snap on my chest rig. "That's one for the good guys."

Aurora cleared her throat, and I felt my face flush.

"That's one for the good folks?" I said.

Aurora wrapped her arm around my neck and pulled me until our temples touched.

"Just fucking with you," she whispered.

Five

The last of the little supply boats disappeared over the horizon as the sun peeked over the waves of the Mediterranean. The boatmen scurried away before they fell victim to Ottoman cannons or sharpshooters. When the supplies had stopped altogether for a few days, we pleaded with de Valette, our Grandmaster, to let us withdraw, to let us run. The defense of Fort St. Elmo was long since over. There were barely any walls standing. We had repelled the Janissaries, the Sultan's elite shock troops, day after day for a week. I had broken three dagger blades off in enemy necks. There were, however, so many dead that a convenient supply of weapons was always at hand.

De Valette had said we must hold. Reinforcements were coming from Sicily, and we had to delay the enemy long enough to allow these troops to arrive. So, hold we did. The Ottomans fell ten to each one of ours, but they seemed to have an inexhaustible supply. Their corpses made more of a wall than the remnants of our castle, and as they climbed over their own dead, we fell back inch by inch toward the sea.

The gruesome dance would start up again very soon.

Jude was fishing something brown and mushy out of a pocked apple with his dagger.

"Today's the day, brother," he said.

"Or tomorrow," I replied. "Either way, we'll be starting again soon."

Jude nodded. He was too tired to do anything else.

The Ottomans under Dragut had reduced our fort's wall to boulders, then stones, then pebbles. The fort was no more than a patch of rubble on the tip of the Sciberras Peninsula. Fort St. Elmo would soon be nothing but a graveyard.

And yet.

The day was starting in such vivid blues, the sky, the water. Gulls complained above us but feasted wherever there were no men to shoo them away. Our death was coming from the land behind us, but for this moment, we looked to the sea. The sun was warm against my closed eyes, and I tried to sit perfectly still for ten heartbeats, then twenty.

"I was only fifteen when I died in my last life," Jude said, now using the dagger to pick his teeth, then sliding it into his belt. "I thought I'd make thirty at least this time."

"The good die young," I said, grabbing his hand. I was only twenty-two and still a virgin in this incarnation. I had been raised among the Hospitallers, then newly arrived in Malta from their retreat from Rhoades. They told me my mother had died in childbirth, and they had taken me in. They taught me to read, again, and trained me in the sword until Peter awakened me, and my real fighting skills returned. I had seen action as a Hospitaller pirate, raiding Suleiman the Magnificent's fleet all the way to Tripoli.

"Did you hear about Dragut?" Jude asked, referring to the Ottoman general. "There's a rumor he got hit with one of his own cannonballs." Jude's mouth curled on one side.

"Simon got to their cannons?" I asked, shaking my head with awe.

"He's the best with gunpowder," Jude said. "He's been messing with their cannons for weeks, but they still stomped us into the ground."

"They have a lot of cannons," I said, clearing my throat.

"Today's the day," Jude said again.

Jude and I had gotten lots of wounded soldiers and townsfolk away from the fort to the relative safety of Fort St. Angelo, with cannons of its own. Those ambulance missions ended with our orders to hold Fort St. Elmo at all cost. The men of the fort, not just the brothers or the knights, fought like badgers at the door to their den. Those days in early June, Jude recited from "Thermopylae," by Simonides, urging us to "boundless honor and eternal fame."

We had been worn to nubs in the ensuing battles, and now gave thanks for those with whom we "stood side by side and fought together and together died."

Peter had been killed by a sharpshooter while on the battlements at Fort St. Michael. Andrew was at work in the village of Mdina. He would create an illusion that bluffed the enemy horde into a retreat from the tiny band of ill-equipped soldiers in the town. But we wouldn't hear about that for another twenty years, because by the time Andrew worked his magic, we were in the Ether waiting to be reborn.

I pounded out a dent in my helmet with the pommel of my dagger and cinched it down tight. Then I tightened my sword belt.

"You want to take a bath and shave first?" Jude asked, scowling at my fastidious preparation. He roared, unsheathed his sword, and ran toward the soldiers cresting a stack of bodies, their scimitars raised, a war prayer on their lips.

Part Two: August, Three Months Before the Election.

Six

Washington, DC.

I was on the metro red line, coming into the city from Takoma, Maryland, where I rented an apartment for my now-finished contract, when two young men riding further up the train lunged at each other and began punching. I let go of the standing pole and raised my hand. All motion in the compartment stopped. The train kept going, and passengers in other cars were free to move around the cabin.

I walked around a middle-aged woman whose face was frozen in fright. She was hunched over and jumping to escape the melee. An elderly man beside her held his aluminum cane in front of him like a cudgel. I twisted him to the right so I could get by.

One of the young men, a white guy, had a tee shirt on that said, "Only White Lives Matter." The other guy was not a white guy.

The wise and diplomatic thing to do would have been to de-escalate the situation. To talk reason to them in order to bring about a peaceful resolution.

But there's just no reasoning with that level of bigotry.

As the train slowed for the Judiciary Square stop, I reanimated everyone, except the guy in the offensive tee shirt. He stood stock-still while the non-white guy hit his face with an impressive three-punch combination. Before he could land more punches, I stepped between them and reanimated the wannabe Klansman.

His nose and mouth sprayed a veritable fountain of blood on my *really expensive* leather bomber jacket before he collapsed on the now-empty bench. I suppose that's what I get for leaving wisdom and diplomacy behind. I nodded to the non-white guy who nodded back and scooted out the door just before it closed.

In the brief ride to the hub at Gallery Place, I made sure Mr. White Lives didn't choke on his own blood. I helped him to his feet and half dragged him to a bench in the station.

"You're going to want to put some ice on that," I said before pushing through the turnstiles.

It was rainy, but warm, and my jacket was already ruined, so I walked the few blocks to St. George's Hospital, where my striking colleagues were somberly pacing back and forth, holding up signs, and trying not to take the bait from passersby. The people on the street were having a creative insult contest.

The strike tent had coffee, always a plus, and the signs were printed, not just magic marker, which gave the whole affair a professional touch. The nurses here hadn't had a pay raise in three years since they had first organized the union. They had been working without a contract for six months, and they alleged that management wasn't bargaining in good faith.

Of course they weren't.

These jumped-up petite bourgeoisie thought they invented the art of playing hardball with the help. I remember when the liege lord could have you flogged for eating one of his turnips. This relatively new country thought, like most toddlers, that all its conflicts were new and groundbreaking. The gentry oppressing workers for demanding better pay, or any pay, this was new? Chinese nobles were doing this before John the Baptist was a twinkle in Zechariah's eye. Whenever I hear a reporter say, "For the first time in history," I want to tell him to read a book for heaven's sake.

I did not share my colleagues' ebullience. Most of the time, the downtrodden got trodden further down. I tried to be cautiously enthusiastic.

Alma handed me a sign.

"Aren't you a traveler? Why are you on the picket line?"

"I walk to support the forces of righteousness," I said. "My contract's over, and I think you guys are getting a raw deal. Don't make it a thing."

At the far end of the picket line, away from the tent and the reporters, two men, I'll call them Tweedledee and Tweedledumb (yes, I know that's not how it's spelled), were leaning into a conversation with one of the nurses. She was someone I had worked with in oncology, Erica. She was red-faced, and her body language was daring Dee and Dumb to come closer.

Dee was an old soldier; he sported a crew cut and walked like he had a stick up his ass. Where Dee was whippet thin, Dumb was, well, large. His largeness, in fact, was trying to escape his badly sized clothes. Dumb had a beard and mustache so thick it completely hid his mouth. The spittle he was ejecting seemed to materialize already in motion from the middle of all that hair. And, of course, he wore a Roosevelt hat.

"Your days are numbered," Dumb was saying. "You and your pinko lesbo friends. When our boy gets in, you'll be back cleaning bedpans and glad to get minimum wage for it."

"I already clean bedpans, you ignorant shit," Erica shot back. "And give all the medicines, and comfort the families, and do hours of paperwork. That's the point. That's why we're here. And why do morons like you always assume that any woman who doesn't agree with him must be a lesbian? I weep at the idea that any woman has to put up with *you*. We women should get together and make sure that idiots like you never reproduce."

Walk away, Paul, walk away. She's got this covered.

Dee reached into his pocket, but before his hand emerged, Erica had covered his face in pepper spray. He reeled back, his palms rubbing his eyes, which, of course, made the pain worse. With Dee out of it,

40

Dumb leaped forward, arms outstretched, but the ground buckled under his feet, and he sprawled hard on the pavement. Immediately, a scrum of nurses hit him with their signs. He put his hands over his head and tried to rise, but it was as if the tarmac had hold of his boots.

Weird, huh?

It's a miracle that nobody got really hurt that day. The Green Brigade, a pro-union militia (also a few sandwiches short of a picnic, but they were vegan sandwiches, so . . .), arrived later in the morning and created a barrier between the street and the picket line. Cars and trucks slowed as they passed. Many of the people in those cars yelled hateful things at the protesters, but there were some honks and thumbs-up signs, too. Cans were thrown, minor scuffles broke out. The sides kept at it until well after midnight, when the cops told everyone to go home.

The protesters packed up their things, but the rabble beyond the Green Brigade didn't move, and the police didn't do anything to make them move.

It had been drizzling all day, so there was no surprise when I made thunder rumble over the whole downtown. Then I made it pour, and the crowd dispersed.

There was still a little blood on the bench where I had left Mr. White Lives, but he was gone. A woman in a white sundress waited further down the platform, which reminded me that I had a church gig this weekend, that life was not always screaming and flailing. I was going to perform a marriage for an old friend, a nurse I had worked with several times. She and her fiancé had asked, and I was flattered. I had to get one of those internet ordinations, and the irony was not lost on me. The Order of St. John didn't even convey the authority to perform a wedding nowadays.

After all the vitriol at the picket line, though, I still got on the subway feeling helpless and ineffectual.

I knew this kind of helpless. It's how I felt when I had been unable to stop the pogrom in Odessa. I was the only knight in Russia when the riot started, and the memory of it still haunts me. I could see it all erupting, slowly at first, then an explosion. The forces at work were so violent that I was swept away in the first hours. My day on the picket line felt like an omen, an echo of Odessa. Not the best state of mind to bind two people in love.

Seven

Old Forge, New York.

January Alves was the kind of nurse I aspired to be. Sometimes I
made it, sometimes not, but for January, compassion was as
integral to her person as breathing. I had been the preceptor for
her senior nursing practicum. She was in her last semester of
school, and she had to work twenty hours a week under my supervision
as part of her degree program.

In our first week together, I was buzzing around, day shift,
nonstop, like you do, and I realized I hadn't seen her in half an hour.
Most student nurses follow their preceptors like a shadow, so losing a
student was pretty novel. Some preceptor. If I couldn't even keep track
of her, how could I teach her anything?

I found her in a patient's room. The patient was a young woman,
about her age, who had been paralyzed in a skiing accident. The girl
had been a vagabond, a ski bum. She was out with some friends, skiing
by the light of a full moon while the resort she worked for was closed.
A cloud passed over the moon, the slope went dark, she hit a tree, and
her life changed forever.

The patient had long dreads and several facial piercings. She also
had a case of *Pediculus humanus*, body lice. I have spent decades infested
with body lice in my previous incarnations, just a part of life back in the

43

day. Modern folks, though, they kind of lose their minds over it.

So it was with the nurses on the floor. This poor soul's call bell took forever to be answered, because everyone was hoping that someone else would answer it. Our patient was on "contact precautions," which meant we had to wear a disposable gown and gloves whenever we were near her nest. Nurses call proximity to a patient and their living space the patient's nest.

I found January deep in the patient's nest, sitting right next to her, gowned and gloved, holding her hand. They were laughing at something I couldn't hear. The other student nurses on the floor followed their preceptors around or looked at their phones or books when they weren't with a patient. January wanted to befriend her patient, to make the patient feel cared for and valued.

The best nurses I have known were like this. Some had this surfeit of grace beaten out of them by their daily trials on the floor (and sometimes by their burned-out colleagues), but January's compassion grew and matured. She was the one I wanted to take care of me and my loved ones.

She had fallen in love with a sailor. Historically, sailors have always done well with the ladies. At first, I was skeptical. If I'm being totally honest, I didn't think anyone would be good enough for January, but Alan turned me around. He was, without a doubt, a fearsome warrior. He had the look of someone who had done hard physical work: long, wiry, flat muscles. And he had the eyes of someone who has seen combat, a look I know all too well.

He adored January. He was kind and thoughtful, and despite my initial misgivings, he was the right guy for her.

So, on a gorgeous August day, on a mountain near Old Forge, New York, I was riding a ski lift, dressed to the nines. My date, a midwife who worked at St. Luke's, closed her eyes and let the wind blow through her graying hair whenever the lift stopped, and our chair swung high above the trail below. Leah was wearing a green dress twenty years out-of-date, and she looked fabulous.

"Penny for your thoughts," I said.

"I'm composing my will," she replied.

"You're missing the most wonderful view."

"There's a little movie running in my head where the cable overhead snaps and we plummet. I stop and hit rewind before crashing."

"Ah," I said. "Why didn't you tell me you were afraid of heights?"

"I didn't want you to think I'm a sissy."

The chair started moving again, and she opened her eyes.

"I can deal with it better when we're moving, oddly enough," she said.

I squeezed her hand.

"I saw a lot of Roosevelt signs in town. Will that make your friend uncomfortable?" Leah asked.

"No," I replied. "January is a Roosevelt supporter."

Leah's jaw dropped, and she squeezed the safety bar until her knuckles turned white.

"Please tell me you're joking," she said.

"Nope. She doesn't like the racial stuff, but she's marrying a military guy, and Roosevelt is promising to up pay in the military. Also, she's afraid someone is going to take away her guns."

"They always say that," Leah huffed. "Nobody ever does. It's just a dog whistle."

"Maybe," I conceded, "but you would if you could."

"Of course I would. I thought you would, too."

"Sure," I said. "I would put all kinds of limits on guns. My point is just that she isn't wrong to think that. I don't understand it any more than you do. You know what I think of Roosevelt. But this is January. She might be misinformed, but she doesn't want to hurt anyone."

"I wish I could be so sure," Leah said, grabbing my arm as the safety bar lifted, and we hopped off the chair.

January was waiting for me. People say, "she glowed," but that's so overused, and usually inaccurate, in my experience. January really did glow, as if her face was being lit from within. She wrapped me up in a bear hug.

"You didn't think I would forget?" I asked, only half smirking.

"Of course not. I'm just glad to see you. Alan's with his family, but he really wants to say hi before the ceremony."

I introduced January to Leah. Then I met her parents. Yes, I was a preacher (with air quotes). No, I did not belong to any church they would recognize. I could tell from Mom's expression that she was not happy with this, but you can't please all the people, etc.

I heard a step behind me, and before I could turn around, I got another bear hug. It was funny how Alan and January both hugged the same way, with abandon. They squeezed too hard and held on too long and it was the best.

"Brother Paul," he said, steering me away from his soon-to-be in-laws. No one outside of the Order ever called me that. It brought me up short for a moment before I realized that he was just making fun of my internet ordination.

"Good energies upon thee," I replied, reaching up to touch the top of his head with my palm. "May your chakras all exceed their factory warranty and your lights be properly polarized."

"Amen," he responded solemnly. "You doing okay? Jan's folks can be a little intense."

I smiled.

"They were just fine. You set?"

"Seems like this is where I have been headed all along. Jan is the part I have been missing my whole life."

"That's wonderful," I said, patting his shoulder.

"The politics aren't too much, I hope," he said, and there was such nervous anticipation in his voice, it evoked a twang of guilt. He was so worried I might be offended. "I know you're a lib—"

"—tard," I finished. "I'm not really, though. Those terms, liberal and conservative, they have little meaning without context."

Alan's brow knitted.

"One man's liberal is another's conservative. Republicans were the progressives, once. Movements change over time. Anyway, I'm a nurse, I don't want anybody to go without care or medicine. I want the embedded discrimination to end. Does that make me a libtard?"

"Depends on who you ask," he said.

I nodded. It did, indeed.

"Between you and me," Alan said, looking around, "I'm not voting for Roosevelt. For god's sake don't tell Jan."

I motioned sealing my lips.

They exchanged vows under a trellis, with precious little guidance from me. The officiant really doesn't do anything at a wedding. It's the power of the bond between the couple and the love of the assembled people for them that work the magic, not any words from a guy in robes, or a cheap suit, for that matter.

Leah and I sat at a table with strangers who also seemed uncomfortable with some of the talk going on around us. The only person of color at the wedding sat with us. He tried to look bored, but there was tension written all over him. Leah did not have a good time.

A figure I thought I recognized navigated through the buffet line toward the bride and groom. He smelled (metaphorically) like one of the Returned, but I didn't recognize him. He leaned toward the happy couple and said something, belly-laughing at the end of his little speech.

January rose, shaking the table, her face red, and pointed away from the reception. Alan rose more slowly, but with impressive menace. The man shook his head and ambled away.

"I know that guy," Leah said under her breath. "He's the congressman for this district, big Roosevelt supporter."

"January and Alan didn't think much of him," I said. "That's reason to hope."

Eight

Leah and I drove in silence, or rather, she drove, while I was deep in thought. Why was a sitting congressman giving off a Returned vibe? It was hardly surprising that Upstate New York had a congressman who supported Roosevelt. The odd, and terrifying, thing was that the Returned's influence was flowing down to local races. Roosevelt hadn't been elected to any office, but he had coattails, as the politicians put it. Or was this congressman part of the Returned's grand strategy? Perhaps they had promised him power in their brave new world. That meant they were confident that Roosevelt would win. The fix was in, but I didn't know how.

"Gotta say, Paul," Leah began, "I'm a little disappointed."

"Oh?"

"That was a bunch of Hitler Youth back there. I can't understand why you would agree to do their wedding."

"Hey," I said, "there are real Hitler Youth in this country now. Don't let your polemic carry you away. I told you, Jan is a great nurse, one in a million, and Alan confided in me that he's not voting for Roosevelt."

"And you believe him?"

"Yes, I believe him. What's gotten into you?"

Leah sighed. She had told me once how midwives have to be

completely nonjudgmental. They preside over some awful situations. She told me that if she were to let her feelings about a drug-addicted mom affect her care in any way, she would lose maybe the only opportunity to do something positive for the baby, maybe the only opportunity to educate the mother. Their well-being mattered more than her sensibilities. The Leah I was talking to now was different from the caring midwife. This Leah was really scared. Roosevelt and his ilk were shattering her view of the world.

"Nobody innocently votes for Roosevelt," she said with a low snarl. "He's right up front about his bigotry and his disdain for democracy. You'd have to be pretty stupid not to see that. Or you'd have to be complicit in his bullshit."

"It's us and them," I said. As soon as the words left my mouth, I knew she was probably right, but I couldn't think of January as the enemy. Was January being naive about Roosevelt, or was I being naive about January?

"You're goddamn right," Leah replied.

At that moment I knew three things: (1) I had to contact headquarters right away about the corrupted congressman, (2) I would have to have a long think about January's politics, and (3) I was definitely not getting laid that night.

My leave-taking the next morning was painfully awkward, but I was on a plane to South Carolina by ten o'clock, a broken friendship behind me. The shocking part was that we agreed on the issues, and yet an important bond between us had been irreparably damaged.

In-flight newscasts told me that after initially decrying Roosevelt's positions on race and gender equality, many of the members of his party were falling in line with endorsements. Some of the party's elder statesmen were endorsing a candidate I doubt they would have invited into their homes. The flushing sound of many political careers would be metaphorically deafening if Roosevelt lost.

Peter and James were in the Great Hall when I arrived. They were watching cable news, and they both looked shaken.

"Senator Donahue has endorsed Roosevelt," Peter murmured.

"There must be magic at play," James said. "I can't believe Donahue would be campaigning for a bigot."

"I saw some of that in New York," I said.

"I read your report, Paul. The dominoes are falling all of a sudden, and we don't know why," Peter said.

"Dark magic," James said again.

"Maybe," I allowed. "The magic may not be so direct, though. Mind-controlling so many people would take more mojo than the Returned have in this plane. They have found some way to speak directly to ignorance and resentment. It's like what they did in Tulsa."

The Returned had been behind the genocide in Tulsa, Oklahoma, in 1921. Black Wall Street had improved fortunes of Black people all over the United States. It was becoming a beacon, a place that might one day be a cornerstone of Black finance and capital. There was simmering jealousy and race hatred in Tulsa before the riot, but Lilith herself, the Returned's chief operating officer, used a human vessel to invent a charge of assault against a Black man. The Returned-controlled newspaper gave the story inflammatory coverage, and that's all it took. The beast inside those people was turned loose. They destroyed that entire section of town. There was never a final casualty count.

The mayhem was short-lived, but the Returned had obviously learned a lesson. The election of a Black president fanned embers that the Returned could exploit. Now Roosevelt would turn that smoldering spark into a conflagration that would allow the Ether to open fully. If they were using magic at all, it was to get their message out, to normalize the craziest of the crazies, giving everyone permission to indulge their worst angels.

"We have been outflanked," Peter said simply.

"I do not accept that people would behave this way without magical influence," James said, his voice flat.

Peter drew his mouth into a thin line but said nothing.

"What can we do now?" I asked. "At least some of those who don't support Roosevelt are terrified, and Roosevelt continues to bait them. We can't be far from violence."

"Clearly not," Peter said. "When we eliminated Gilchrist, we thought we had cut off the beast's head, but now a greater beast rises."

"Might have been the plan all along," I said. "Maybe they played us. I doubt it, but they have plans within plans."

"It's true that Gilchrist didn't put up much of a defense. Could he have known we were coming for him? Could he have known that we would send Aurora?" James asked.

"That would imply we have another traitor in our midst," Peter replied.

"Anything is possible," I said. "But I think we're succumbing to the general paranoia. We don't know for certain they had any idea we would strike them at the convention.

"Nonetheless," Peter said, "we should change the wards around headquarters, maybe go to regular patrols at night."

"That won't help us if the problem is within our gate already," James said. He never showed much emotion, but the way his heel thumped under the table, I knew he was wound up.

Before I could form a comforting reply, Miguel burst into the room.

"*Disculpe*, Peter," Miguel said, breathless, "but this is urgent. Thomas is in the ICU and they just called. They say the family should come right away if they want to say goodbye."

Nine

Thomas's dark skin was sallow under the harsh lights. I turned off the overhead light, which made him look only marginally better. He reached his hand out to take mine, the bruises from previous IV tubes and blood draws running from his knuckles to his elbow. When your liver is failing, you get a lot of bruising.

"Does it hurt much?" I asked.

"Remember the *Mahmudiye*?"

Back in our pirate days, we screwed up and took a run at a Turkish warship. It was suicidal, which we didn't realize until they turned *toward* us. We thought they were a supply vessel. Instead, we had aroused the interest of the largest ship in the Ottoman fleet. Thing was huge, more than a hundred guns, if I remember right. We tried to run, but the behemoth was also fast, which was really unfair. She caught us and let one cannon volley loose, just the one. It tore through us like a fork through clotted cream.

Thomas was hit with not one but two cannon balls. The first one took out both of his legs below the knee. He would have bled to death in agony from that wound, but in one of those moments that makes me absolutely sure there is no god, another shot took out his right arm at the shoulder right on the heels of the first round.

It took him a full thirty seconds to die, but lord, it must have felt like a lifetime. I was pulled out of the water later and beheaded, which was a much better way to go.

"That much pain?" I asked, sitting on the side of the bed.

A wide smile bloomed in the wreckage of his sallow face.

"Psych," he replied, and I started to cry. I was the last of the family to see him. Aurora was out west on assignment and wouldn't get home in time, but everyone else had stood where I was now, one by one.

"Paul," he said, wincing, "they have all been too polite to say it, but you can't wait for me to grow up once I've been reborn. The crisis now requires all of us if we have any hope of surviving it."

"You don't need to worry about that now, brother. That won't be your burden again for a while."

Thomas's eyes rolled back into his head with the effort of speaking.

"Garridan Roosevelt is Thaumiel," he whispered.

You think having to say goodbye to one of your best friends is awful. Then you find out that the CEO and chairman of the board of directors of evil might become the leader of the free world. Never say "It couldn't get worse." You're just asking for trouble.

Thomas flexed his hand on mine, and I bent close to his mouth. "Dakar. Quarterstaff. You decide, Paul. Only you."

Those were his last words.

We drove back to headquarters in silence. Aurora was waiting for me at Cambridge House when I got there. Her eyes were red with crying, and she hugged me limply, bending a little to lay her head on my shoulder. I stroked her curls, which were forever trying to ensnare my fingers.

"I'm sorry, Dad," she said. "I'm going to miss him, too."

"So say we all," I replied. "You go get settled, and then you can help me with something."

Aurora lived at the other end of our compound now, in a stone cottage with a thatch roof, Quito House, Jude's old home. She touched her forehead to mine and shuffled off. Her walk spoke volumes about her feelings. Aurora never dragged her feet. She sprang and darted wherever she went.

There were several news alerts on my phone, all telling me that Roosevelt had pulled ahead in some battleground states. I didn't have the time or emotional energy to read them, so I dropped my jacket and tie in the living room, doffed the rest of my funeral clothes, and flopped onto the bed for another long cry.

I was dressed in a black tee shirt and khakis when Aurora arrived. I said nothing but headed directly to Thomas's house. It was a testimony to her trust in me that Aurora also said nothing; she just followed without any explanation. I had a key to the decorative iron gate around Dakar House, and another for the second gate into the veranda.

The house was, as ever, perfect: orderly, clean, tasteful. Two straw mats with interwoven leather spanned the veranda, cushions and long mattresses on each of them. At the side of one mat were a charcoal brazier and ornate metal teapot, beside them a tray with tea glasses. The inside of the house was cool, white concrete reflecting light from the low windows. It was a house made for sitting on the floor.

The veranda opened onto a single large room, square with a ceiling four meters high. The teak fan on the ceiling was motionless, the only movement in the room the dust motes in shafts of sunlight. On the wall opposite the door were hung several traditional weapons, a saber, a rapier, an assortment of knives and daggers, and, in the middle, a rack of quarterstaffs. I knew immediately which one to take.

The rosewood staff shone. It had been polished to a high gleam by Thomas's hands. In nine hundred years he had studied the martial arts of the staff in many disciplines, aikido, jujitsu, the London school, even old texts with spear techniques used by the Roman legions. Thomas had a modern armory hidden below the main building in Dakar, but his real love, if a man's primary weapon is ever loved, was the staff.

"Why that one?" Aurora asked. "Two of the others are enchanted or were. They have runes along their lengths."

"This was his favorite, the first one he picks up when he is awakened. He has remade it with magic when it breaks. There's a lot of him in this wood. If he was going to hide something, he would put it in here."

"There's something inside the staff?"

I nodded.

"I don't know yet what it is," I said. "I want you here in case it's dangerous."

Now Aurora nodded. I handed her one end of the staff, while I held the other. Putting my thumb and forefinger around the middle, I rotated my hand, and a red circle appeared and flared. When the flare went out, the staff was neatly cut in half. Aurora and I pulled the ends away from each other. By the time we got a meter apart, we knew that nothing bad was going to happen, at least not from cutting the staff.

I flipped my end around. It was hollow, the interior so black it swallowed the light around it. I put it up to my eye to peer in, and suddenly I was blind.

I was also no longer in Dakar House. The floor beneath me was bowed and smooth, as were the walls and the low ceiling.

I was in the staff. A tiny flame appeared before me. It grew into an archway. I walked through to find Thomas sitting on a bench beside a noisy little brook.

"So glad you got my message," Thomas said, without rising.

"Your dying words," I replied.

"Lot of magic in those," Thomas said. "Tough to get the timing right, but very powerful if you can. So I died of . . .?"

"Multiple organ failure. The heart first, but then the liver went, too."

"Hmm. Not surprised, I guess."

"You used up too much life on the ritual for Aurora," I said. My eyes swelled, but I didn't let the tears drop.

"You would have done the same," Thomas said, and he smiled his most radiant smile.

"So, what's this all about?" I asked.

Thomas's face grew serious.

"By now I've told you that Thaumiel is Garridan Roosevelt. The Big Bad is poised to bring his whole world over. We can't afford to be without every knight." He paused. "I have found a way to accelerate my return from the Ether, but you may have some reservations."

"What reservations could I possibly have? We need you most of all if Thaumiel is in this plane."

"I think I can duplicate the method the Returned use to come into this world, to inhabit a host. If we can find one willing, I could take over that body," Thomas said, not looking at me.

"Same effect on the host's spirit? Limbo while you're in there and then death?"

"I'm afraid so," he said. "I haven't told anyone else about this. I trust your judgment to decide if the ends justify the means in this case. If you think it's wrong, I'll just have to come back the usual way."

"How long do I have to decide?" I asked.

"You have to do it before I'm reincarnated," he replied.

"So, today. I have to decide this and find a vessel today."

"I'm sorry," Thomas said. Then he turned to dust, and I was back in Dakar House holding half of his rosewood staff.

"Did you get what you needed?" Aurora asked, her face full of anxiety.

"If only," I replied. "We need to get the whole council together right now."

Ten

It was evening when we assembled in the Great Hall. An empty chair sat at the far corner of the table, next to Bart. Aurora took her place at the end of the table opposite Peter. She had changed so much from the angry teenager who had stuck her tongue out at Augustine at that very table. She was a warrior and a nurse. In her brief time as a knight, she had taken a life, and, as a nurse, she had saved a life. Although I knew my little girl was in there somewhere, she was now something much more.

We recited our oath in monotone murmurs. We drank to Thomas, then Peter rose.

"Shall we have our remembrances of our late brother now? Is that why you called us here, Paul?" he said.

"My lord," I replied. Sure, it was much too formal, since we were among only the Knights of the Order, but I wanted to impress them all with the gravity of what I was about to say. Besides, Peter lives for this kind of thing.

"Brother Paul," he said with a slight bow. "You have the floor."

I looked the table up and down, making a mental note to compliment Aurora on her poker face.

"Thomas was a sorcerer to the very end," I began. "He timed his death so that his last words would be for me and that my magic would ignite a tiny portion of his spirit left behind in one of his staffs."

The knights did not freeze. That would be the province of ordinary people. They *stilled*.

"Before he died, he was able to ascertain the identity of Garridan Roosevelt."

Peter looked like he already knew and didn't want his suspicions confirmed. Augustine looked grim.

"It's Thaumiel, then," Augustine said. I let the name hover among us for a moment before nodding.

"The most powerful, the most ruthless, the most cunning of the Returned is in our world and could seize the ultimate political power," I said.

"I should have seen this coming," Augustine said. "I badly underestimated them."

"We all did, sister," Peter said. "No one will lay this at your doorstep."

"I'm just gonna state the obvious," Simon said, looking at the table. "Without Thomas, we don't stand a chance. Even together, we're not powerful enough to beat him in combat, much less beat him at politics."

"Which brings me to what I saw inside Thomas's staff."

"Was it a girl?" Andrew asked.

That stopped me cold, really cold, like an ice cube running down my spine.

"A what?" I croaked.

"James has talked to me about a recurring dream with a little girl being led away by something evil."

"It's true," James said. "It has the feeling of prophecy."

"We have been having the same dream," Bart said, Phil nodding in agreement.

"Have we all been having this dream?" Peter asked.

All of them nodded, except Aurora.

"I'm having a different dream," she said. "There's a little girl, but she's snuggled under this giant bird, like a swan or an ostrich or something. She's curled up in the fetal position with the bird's body all around her. Then I hear the sound of one of those old-fashioned clocks. You know, the ones with the bird that pops out?"

"A cuckoo clock," Peter said.

"Yeah," Aurora said, snapping her fingers, "a cuckoo clock."

"In my dream, she's led away by a surgeon who is really being a prick," I admitted. "But I've only seen that once."

"Was the little girl in Thomas's staff?" James asked.

"No," I said. "It was just Thomas. He's found a way to come back to us right away, but he needs a willing vessel to do it, and we have to find one tonight, before he is reborn."

Conversation erupted around the table, so loudly that Peter drummed his knuckles on the table.

"Paul has the floor," he said, and the others quieted.

Augustine stood up. I nodded at her, allowing her to speak.

"Even if this were possible, and I doubt it, and we could find a vessel, which we can't, we have to decide if it's right to do so. The council will have to debate the issue."

"I'm sorry, Augustine, but that's not true. Thomas left it for me to decide."

"He can't—" she said, loudly, but my raised hand cut her off.

"His dying words were that only I could decide," I said. The room was now so quiet that I did not have to raise my voice.

Augustine glowered, but she sat down. None of us would deny a knight his final request.

"Thomas's instructions contained the information I need to make this work. That leaves the problem of a vessel."

The back door to the hall creaked as it opened. We turned as one to see Miguel's head sticking through the opening.

"May I come in?" he asked.

"I'm sorry, son," Peter said. "This is not a good time."

"I will be Thomas's vessel."

"Absolutely not," Peter said.

Miguel moved all the way into the room.

"I have been living on borrowed time for years," he said. "I should have died back in the container truck with my parents when I was little. And you saved me after I was shot and left for dead, too. I know I don't have any magic, but I can do this, at least. I can help."

"You don't know what we're asking," I said.

"I do," Miguel replied. "The worst of the Returned might become president, and you can't fight him without Thomas."

"You were eavesdropping?" Peter's disappointment was uncharacteristically plain on his face.

"I understand that I won't ever come back once Thomas has my body. Without Thomas, it doesn't sound like we'll have a world worth returning to. I am a soldier, too. Maybe not a knight or a nurse or a sorcerer, but I can do this. Please," Miguel said plaintively.

Augustine also looked plaintive, but she was imploring me not to allow Miguel to become Thomas's vessel. Augustine is much smarter than I am. James has foresight. Andrew understands the depths of the human psyche, but Thomas left the decision to me.

"Very well," I said at last. I looked at Miguel's hopeful face, his resolve and his courage written plain. "We will bring Thomas back tonight."

Peter turned his head away, and sobs wracked his shoulders. I hadn't realized until that moment how much like a son Miguel had become to him.

Eleven

Peter was still grieving the loss of Miguel a week later. All of the knight-nurses were on a first-name basis with loss and grief, Peter more than most because his lives were so long, but the business with Miguel was different. Peter blamed himself for not protecting Miguel, while at the same time, as our leader, understanding that without Thomas we couldn't hope to stop the Returned.

And so, Thomas had taken over Miguel's body. Honestly, it was creepy how easy it was. I knew immediately that it would be simple to do it more often, and that it would corrupt our order absolutely if we did so. With Peter MIA for the moment, and we still had no battle plan. Augustine is our general, but she won't order a bootlace without talking to Peter.

We did not ride pillars of fire into the night sky, raining death and destruction over the foe, although that would have been wicked cool. We did not execute a brilliant media counterstrike, taking Roosevelt's camp by surprise and cementing the swing voters against him. We were left with the most pedestrian of opposition weapons: leafleting.

I was dividing up stacks of pamphlets for Roosevelt's opponent, while a newscaster mumbled in the background on the radio. Thomas, in his new body, filled a canvas backpack. His new body was considerably smaller than the old one, and whether it was the physical presence or the cost of obtaining it, Thomas was diminished.

"Orange County?" I asked from across the room.

"I drew the short straw," he replied.

"It's not so bad," I said. "Nice and warm down there."

"Bite me," Thomas replied, without looking up. I know he meant it to be funny, but it was sharp and dry. We were all trying too hard to accept Thomas like we had at every other rebirth, but this wasn't like every other rebirth.

"Really?" Augustine said as she came through the door with a bin of pamphlets. "This is what a millennium of experience has brought you to? Acting like a couple of prepubescent boys?"

Thomas and I looked at each other.

"Bite me," we said in tandem.

Augustine inhaled through her nose, a long, fierce breath, closed her eyes, the blew the air out through pursed lips.

"What's shaking, Aunty A?" Aurora asked, entering from the kitchen. She had a sandwich in one hand and a can of soda in the other. This wasn't her usual diet at ten o'clock in the morning. Aurora had an eating disorder that involved binging then purging in several different ways, usually through excessive exercise. She was in charge of herself and her illness, of course, but that didn't stop me from worrying.

Augustine looked at the soda but said nothing.

Simon came in behind Aurora.

"Aunty A's booty, that's what's shakin'. Got some junk in the trunk, Gus," said Simon. "Laugh to keep from crying, am I right? I, on the other hand, look amazing. Say it, I look like I just came back from the spa."

Augustine took another one of those long, slow breaths.

"Has this always been such a boys' club?" Aurora asked.

"Dear girl, you have no idea," Augustine replied.

Aurora looked at her hands and was surprised to see the food.

"Eep," she said. She dropped the sandwich in the trash, opened the window behind her, and poured out the soda, crushing the can when it was empty.

Augustine sighed. She and I shared a look; we would both be keeping an eye on Aurora.

With three boys now in the house and Augustine lecturing us, bad behavior was guaranteed.

"Stop," Augustine commanded. "I know that look between you three. Someone is going to do something stupid, and I don't need that aggravation right now."

We three brothers tried to look chastened. Simon had that look like he was brewing a loud fart. He was really good at being able to do that on command. A flicker of a smile passed over his face, but he went back to sorting pamphlets.

"You really are a saint," Aurora said to Augustine. "I can't believe you have been the only woman for so long." She paused for a moment. "Well, I guess there have been times when you weren't."

"Oy," Simon called. "You're going to jinx me. I really can't go through that again."

"Poor baby," Augustine said with mock sympathy. "In the early days, before Jerusalem and Ibn Jamay, there were lots of women. We were an Augustinian order; they were open to women. Lots of the nurses were women in the eleven hundreds."

"But all of the knights were men, right? The ones who died in Jerusalem, the original ten?"

A round of general throat-clearing swept the room.

"I was one of the ten, and I was in a male body back then," Augustine agreed. "In point of fact, though, one of the original ten was female."

"He doesn't like us to talk about it," I added.

"And we shouldn't," Thomas said. "I keep telling him that we have pronouns for this now, he should just be they/them, but he won't hear of it, too old-fashioned."

"Why am I learning all this in bits and pieces?" Aurora asked. "Why didn't you guys tell me stuff like this up front?"

"We've never had a new knight, dear," Augustine said. "We have shared history for centuries. Honestly, it's hard to keep track of what *you* don't know."

"It's James," I said, enduring the scowls of the rest of them. "He was a Spanish noblewoman from the original house for women Hospitallers in Sigena. Her name then was Ermengarda. She cut her hair short and dressed as a man. She had armor, and she was good in a fight, and she was wonderful with patients, so we carried on with pretending. We didn't really have any other choices back then. If she was openly female, she could have been a Hospitaller, but not a knight. She was male in her first reincarnation, but she is often reborn as a woman. When she is a woman, her name is Perpetua."

"Wow," Aurora whispered.

"James is the reason I want to be reborn as a woman, at least once," Thomas said. "His magic is unique among us. He understands modern life best among us. Whatever the age, James or Perpetua masters the technology and teaches the rest of us. I want to study that ability myself."

"Remember how long it took us to figure out the trebuchet?" Simon asked, looking at me.

"I broke my arm four times before we were done," I replied.

"Why is it such a secret, then?" Aurora asked.

"It's what he wants," Simon replied.

Aurora looked at me and raised an eyebrow.

"I get it, now," she said, looking at me.

I raised one eyebrow in a question.

"Why you didn't think it was such a big deal for me to love another woman. That doesn't even register with you guys."

I shrugged.

"You guys are major pervs," Aurora said and giggled through her nose the way she had when she was little. That brought chuckles all around.

James appeared at the door with yet another bin of pamphlets, and the chuckles turned into full belly laughs.

"What did I miss?" he asked.

Twelve

November 1805, Schöngrabern, Austria

Jude was on his knees in the blood-sodden dirt. His previously white breeches were now indistinguishable from his gray coat. I crawled on my belly to him as a cannonball from the French Fifth Corps whistled overhead then shook the ground behind us. The rich Austrian soil showered on us after the impact, and I used his cloak to grab Jude by the shoulders and pull him a few meters to our left before dropping again to the ground.

His right ear was a swinging lobe, ready to fall in a strong wind. The rest of his ear was gone, and there was so much blood around the side of his head, it looked as if he had taken a blow with an axe. I knew it had been a bullet, because I was beside him when it happened. The lower part of his right arm dangled, yellow-white bone piercing his coat sleeve like a dagger. It must have hurt like white hell whenever I dragged him but drag him I did.

Our unit of Russian infantry had disappeared into the cloud of gunpowder smoke in front of us. Horses nickered in the woods behind us. The battlefield smelled of rancid, burning gunpowder, some made from horse urine. The volume of blood on the field added a metallic aftertaste to each breath. One of the French troops appeared suddenly out of the fog. He seemed surprised to see us there, on the ground. He swung his musket over his shoulder, but before he could level the bayonet, Jude ran him through.

Jude stood, his right arm hanging useless, blood streaming down his face and neck. Another French soldier appeared, and Jude almost decapitated him. The man's dangling head tucked under him when he fell. For long moments, I could only gape. When it finally dawned on me that my half-dead brother was still fighting, I grabbed the first Frenchman's musket, secured the bayonet, and stood beside Jude. We killed twelve men before they stopped coming, and the ground rolled with the hoofbeats of our Prince Bagration's cavalry. When they had passed, Jude collapsed. I carried him over my shoulder back to camp where the barbers who served as our surgeons cut off his arm at the shoulder.

I sat with him that night. He was so pale. Blood seeped into the bandage around his head from his severed ear. I reached out to him to check for a fever when a shadow crossed over us. I turned to see the prince, our general, looking down on us. His aide-de-camp and the rest of his entourage stood back, away from the ghastly wreck of humanity that was laid out in every direction on the ground.

"Your friend fights like a demon. That's what my men say," said the prince, drawing his mouth into a thin line.

"Like an angel, General," I said, "like a wrathful angel."

"Better that you do not blaspheme," he said.

"Better that you do not describe my friend as a creature of darkness, General." I added the last word after a pause.

One of the officers stepped forward and raised a leather glove, but the prince just held up his hand and waved the officer away.

"A wrathful angel, then," said the prince. "Against Napoleon's armies we will need the whole heavenly host."

"Amen," I said.

The prince smiled that grimacing smile of his and patted my shoulder.

Jude was dead before sunrise.

Part Three: September, Two Months Before the Election.

Thirteen

Santa Rosa, New Mexico.

I sat in an empty hospital room watching a documentary about Garridan Roosevelt. It was three in the morning. I only had two patients, both walkie-talkies, and they were both asleep. One of them was an old guy with dementia whose wife would sometimes drop him off at the emergency department, then go home and take her phone off the hook. The other nurses called this "enforced respite care." He really wasn't much trouble, and they all liked the wife and understood that, as a woman in her eighties, taking care of her husband was completely exhausting. In every one of these visits, the doctors were left with the daunting task of coming up with a diagnosis for admission. Tonight, it was "fatigue."

The rural New Mexico hospital where I was working had sent a nurse home because of a lack of patients. I hate it when they do that. The nurse would have to use up vacation time for a day off she hadn't planned. It was a penny-wise, pound-foolish policy to me. The nurses here wouldn't stay long if they couldn't count on steady work and planned days off. My contract said if they called me off, they had to pay me anyway, so I never got called off.

The TV documentary was punctuated with infomercials, half of which were from the Committee to Elect Garridan Roosevelt. He had a super PAC, of course, that sponsored both the commercials and the documentary. It was a documentary in name only; the whole show was a promotion piece, although a casual viewer might mistake it for actual journalism. In my experience, Americans, as a group, were not particularly discriminating consumers of news.

The lone nurse's aide on the floor that night leaned on the doorway into the room where I was sitting. Her arms were crossed, a satisfied smile spreading across her face.

"He's going to bring us back to a Christian nation," she said.

"A what?"

"A Christian country, Paul. That's where we started, but we got lost somewhere."

"Hold up," I said. "You've heard of the separation of church and state? You know like, how we're *not* a Christian nation? No state religion? Ring a bell?"

"Oh," she replied, frowning, "you're one of those."

"Sorry," I said, "one of what?"

"Liberals," she answered. The tone dripped disgust.

"Not really, not by any accurate definition, but I support some of their values."

"Treating all the races equally?"

"Yes," I said, and my spider sense began to tingle.

"Open borders."

"Mostly."

"Free stuff."

"Like what free stuff?" I asked, and the room seemed to grow darker.

"College, healthcare, minimum income."

"Yeah. I think those things should be free." I rolled off the chair and scooted up to the bed just as a blade went whizzing by my right ear. It was a scalpel, a number ten knife, I think. At least it was probably sterile.

"That won't do, knight. That just won't do." The voice that came out of that tiny woman was loud and distorted, like the loudspeakers at a monster truck rally. The bed I used for cover suddenly lifted to smack the ceiling, then rammed down against the floor. It did this four or five times until pieces started falling off. I tried to freeze time, but the little aide shrugged off the spell like shooing a fly.

That was very not good.

A security guard appeared at her side, his Taser drawn. I knew by the way they moved, almost synchronized, that Zaraq was piloting both of them. As a Returned executive, he could be in this plane only in the body of someone who had allowed him in. I had seen him in different vessels in Charleston, when Aurora offed Prentiss Gilchrist. Since no one in my order had reported sending him to the Ether, I had to conclude that he had just thrown away the old vessels, and their former human inhabitants. He was moving from vessel to vessel now and wasting the lives of the people whose bodies he took, like Kleenex. There were enough willing souls now that he could go anywhere, be almost anyone. Which also meant I didn't know how many more people he was using here in the hospital.

The light dimmed steadily, while shadows crawled around me and along the ceiling.

I turned my body completely black; I was like any other black spot in the room, and I glided into the growing shadow. Both aide and security guard shrieked when they lost sight of me. The prongs of the taser lashed out, sparking as they fell to the floor. The aide tried to turn the overhead light on, but the switch toggled with no effect. I borrowed from Aurora's playbook and overloaded the hospital's power. The whole building went dark. An emergency generator would click on momentarily, so I didn't have much time to work.

The Taser was still sparking on the floor. Security guard kept pushing the trigger, like a nervous tic, and the unit would be drained in a second. The oxygen ports over the bed had green taps, but in this light, I could only feel them. I spun them both open all the way, then sprinted to the window. The glass melted away in front of me, and I dove through. I was still maintaining my black camouflage and disintegrating the window when the room exploded behind me. What with the boom and the concentration required for the other workings, I had neglected preparations for a fall.

Good news, only two floors up. Bad news, I was two floors up. There was unearthly screaming from inside the hospital and the heat of fire bursting through the window opening as I fell. I landed on my feet and felt both legs break instantly. The sensation was bad enough, but the sound made me want to puke.

It hurt quite a bit.

I had the presence of mind to release the camouflage spell before I passed out.

Fourteen

My first thought was that I had died. The landscape around me looked an awful lot like the Ether. As my panic rose like bile in my throat, I couldn't breathe. I had let the Order down, and all of our moral sacrifice to bring Thomas back had still left us shorthanded because I was dead. Around me nothing but gray desert and shame. The red feathers of a male cardinal perched nearby changed my mind, though. There is no red in the Ether, or cardinals, for that matter.

A dream, then, or perhaps unconscious musings. I have always dreamed in color, and, over the centuries, have learned quite a bit about conscious dreaming. The cardinal was perched on the branch of a tree that had tight buds on it. The branch hung suspended over a pond where the surface of the water was liquid, but thick, like quicksilver, its banks covered by brown grass and mud.

On the other side of the pond from me, a hill rose so steeply that the ranks of trees along it grew at forty-five degrees to the soil. Shafts of gray rock emerged randomly up the slope, and my eyes followed them to the top where two figures stood out against the iron sky. They were only silhouettes, the weak light behind them obscured any detail. One was tall, the other short as a child. The short figure pulled against the tall figure's hand. It was trying to run down the hill. It was trying to run to me.

I watched this shadow-puppet show, the child tugging toward the slope and the adult pulling her back. I knew, somehow, that the child was a little girl. The tall figure reached its hand back and slapped the child across the head so hard that the child flew backward. She didn't fall, because the tall figure was holding her hand. It pulled her to standing, then hit her again.

I was frantic to get to her. I tried to leap up. I would swim across the pond and run up the hill, but I was sunk to the waist in mud. No matter how hard I tried, I couldn't move my legs. I was frantic, screaming and cursing. Everything I am, everything that I have been, had one purpose, one goal. Get to that little girl.

My eyes flew open, and I tried to sit up, but my arms were in leather restraints. I flailed against them and instantly the pain in my legs took my breath away. From hip to foot, both legs were surrounded by metal rods and pins. The pins went through the skin and into the bone. They're called external fixators, and most commonly used when someone has broken a bone into so many pieces that you need hardware to hold it together while it heals.

A face loomed over me, a silhouette, like in my dream, against the overhead light.

"Easy, Dad," Aurora said, putting her hand on my forehead. "Are you really here this time, or is this another fit?"

I couldn't see her face, and I tried to lift my hand to cover my eyes, but the restraints prevented me. She saw immediately what I needed and reached behind her to switch off the light.

"Better?" she asked as I flopped back against the pillows.

"Where am I?" I asked and started coughing. The bed underneath me whirred, and I was sitting up, clearing my lungs.

"UNM Hospital in Albuquerque. Do you remember anything? The helicopter ride, anything?"

I shook my head,

"How about taking off the restraints?" I asked. "I'm not going to pull anything out or cause trouble."

"Say it first," Aurora said, hands on hips.

"Really?"

"You don't say it, you have to wait for the nurse to take off the restraints."

When she was little and one of us was behind a locked door or otherwise incapacitated, we would say my favorite (everybody's favorite) line from "The Cask of Amontillado." I made Aurora say it every time I bound her up in my "unbreakable hug."

"Fine," I said and sighed. "For the love of God, Montresor." I made the line as desperate and pleading as I could. Given my complete lack of theatrical training, I'm sure it was pathetic and cartoonish. But it got the job done.

Aurora nodded once and unbuckled the leather straps at my wrists.

"Why are these on, anyway? I'm not intubated."

"You were a handful," she replied, releasing the second strap. "You kept trying to get up and walk. You were screaming. Not gonna lie, it was ugly."

This hit close to home.

"I was the Old Maid patient," I said in hushed tones.

"Were you ever," Aurora agreed.

The Old Maid is the card nobody wants, and everyone tries to get rid of.

She sat on the side of the bed.

"What happened back there?" she asked.

"Zaraq happened," I answered. "And they almost had me."

"Zaraq, again? How did they find you?"

"I don't know," I said, "But I'm starting to think that Jude still has some access to headquarters. Either that or . . ." I couldn't finish.

"Or there's another betrayer."

"Or that," I agreed.

"You know," she began, a slow smile crossing her face, "you can use magic to break a fall."

"I had my hands full," I said. "And I forgot that the window I went out was up so high."

"They said the explosion was so hot it disintegrated the glass in the window," she said.

"I did that."

"Figured."

We sat quietly. She massaged my wrists where the restraints had made welts.

"They almost got Simon, too," she said. "He'll tell you the details, but he barely got away. He ended his contract. Said he got mugged and was too scared to go back to the hospital. He spent the next week lurking around it to see if he could identify his attackers, but I guess they had left town, because he didn't see them again."

I asked the question I had been afraid to ask.

"What about you?"

"They haven't tried anything with me," she said, "yet." She looked me over appraisingly. "Are you going to use this time as a vacation? Just gonna lie there? The election is just over a month away."

"I predict a miraculous recovery," I said. "Truly unprecedented in the medical literature."

Fifteen

ndrew picked me up from the hospital. I overdid the healing spell, and part of my left fibula grew so hard around the pins that the surgeon had to use a four-pound sledgehammer to take them out in the operating room. I had no idea that there were sterile sledgehammers, but apparently orthopedic surgeons use them all the time. Thankfully, I was totally out, so I didn't have to hear the *thwang*.

I needed only a cane to get into Andrew's car. We had a long drive back to South Carolina, but he told me he had been working on a self-driving car spell that we could use part of the way home.

"No way," I said, checking to be sure my seat belt was securely fastened.

"I created a construct of me, a semisolid homunculus that knows the rules of the road. It drives while I rest," he said.

"Elon Musk is going to sue you," I said.

"Let him try," Andrew replied.

We got onto the highway and up to cruising speed. Andrew whispered some Latin, then turned toward me.

"Look, Mom, no hands," he said, holding up both arms.

"How old are we?"

He chuckled.

"I heard you and Thomas were harassing the women at HQ." He reached into the back seat and pulled a bag of baby carrots out of his shoulder bag, offered them to me, then started chomping.

"Simon, too," I agreed. "We were all tense about Thomas."

"I'm sorry I couldn't be there," he replied, between chomps.

"What's with the carrots, anyway?" I asked.

"Trying to quit smoking." He answered without looking at me.

"I didn't know you smoked. Since when?"

"Since my last assignment, the one I was on when you resurrected Thomas," he said. "It was, well, I don't think 'harrowing' is too strong a word. It's bad out there, Paul."

"Tell me about it." I pointed to my legs as I said it. "No offense, but you work with locked-unit mental health patients. Isn't it always kinda crazy?" Andrew is our psychiatric nurse specialist, and I knew as soon as I said it, I had screwed the pooch. Also not a great expression.

"I do not like that word, Paul," he replied. It took some effort for him to keep his annoyance in check. "I don't refer to your patients as 'sickos' or 'dead men walking.' You know better than that. But to answer your question, it's bad in a different way. There's a group

88

psychosis out there now. And every nasty, self-serving fantasy that's been repressed in the name of civilization is being turned loose. Not just my patients, I could feel it in the city. I'd go to a movie and people would yell and throw things at the screen. When I went for a drink, fights would break out at the bar. I saw opposing groups of protesters run full tilt at each other brandishing homemade weapons, with the police in the middle."

"They're way out ahead of us this time," I agreed. "Some days I wonder if they haven't already won, if the whole population of the Ether has taken over, jumped into every person in our world."

"The chaos tells you they haven't won yet," Andrew said. "Once they fully take over, there won't be brawls and protests. It will all be under the Returned's control."

"We'll be another branch of the company."

"Exactly," Andrew said. "You're right that we haven't got much time, though. I expect as we get closer to the election, it will get even worse."

I almost said it couldn't get any worse, then I remembered my own advice.

"We also don't have a plan," I said. I ticked off items on my fingers. "We can't assassinate Roosevelt. Thaumiel is too strong and too clever to let us get close enough. He is as good as Thomas in bending reality to his will. His opponent's supporters don't have the same level of energy. I'm not saying we should manipulate them, tempting as it is. But if we did, I don't think we'd get as dramatic a result. I think it would just raise the temperature of the whole conflict."

"What troubles me," said Andrew, "is that Thaumiel hasn't moved directly against us."

"What do you call trying to sink a scalpel into my forehead?" I cried. "And Simon got beat up pretty badly, too."

"I didn't mean to minimize those things."

Always a psych nurse.

"They haven't moved against the Order, the institution of K-Nurses, our headquarters," Andrew amended. "They must know where to find us if they're using Jude. Why haven't they come at us yet?"

"The election is a month away," I said. "They still have time."

Andrew's mouth was full of carrot again, but he held his hand, palm down, next to the steering wheel and drew his fingers into a fist. The car slowed by ten miles an hour.

"Speed trap," he mumbled through the carrots.

"Didn't your mothers ever tell you not to talk with your mouth full?"

"I guess the last few did," he said, spitting carrot crumbs all over me.

"Do you think this, what did you call it, group psychosis, is all magically induced? Are they strong enough to affect that many people?" I asked.

Andrew swallowed and took a drink of water from a metal

container between the seats.

"Thomas doesn't think so," he said. "I'm skeptical, too. It would take a lot of raw power to influence a hundred million people, more than they could bring to bear."

"Maybe they've got some new weapon, some magical device, some way of amplifying their power?"

"Perhaps," Andrew said, pausing to pull at his beard. "But I think the Returned are just making a spark on dry tinder. This hatred and anger have been there. The magic is giving people permission to express it violently and self-righteously. I hate to say it, but the Returned have figured out exactly where to push. A nudge in the right place would take a lot less power than influencing so many people directly."

"So, how do we push back?"

"I don't know that we can. Roosevelt appeals to his followers without reason. He talks to their primitive brain, unloosing all of the restrictions of society, the agreements we all live with in order to have a civilization. He tells them that these compromises, our institutions, aren't the key to prospering and advancing, they are the shackles that hold us back. He's saying that logic and reason are either an illusion, or, if they are real, they don't matter."

"That seems unhealthy to me," I offered.

"It's batshit insane."

Chapter Sixteen

The Ether. After Paul's Death, 1972.

My eyes opened to dim, gray light. I lay naked at the mouth of a cave. The air was neither warm nor cold. The rock beneath me felt smooth, regular. There was a slight breeze.

I rolled onto my haunches and ran my fingers through my hair. It was very long, and judging by the tips, it was brown again. I had returned to my original body, as I did every time I entered the Ether. I backed further into the cave, looking left and right, seeing no one. When K-Nurses are in the Ether, we hide. If someone from the company finds us, brings us to the Returned, our time in the Ether, however brief, will be unceasing agony.

Ain't nobody got time for that.

The cave would be safe for a little while, maybe long enough to shelter me until my next incarnation. I didn't want to get trapped here, though. Sometimes the Returned set sentinels at likely caves. I needed to be sure there was another exit. We were always transported to caves when we died. I don't know why. Maybe it speaks to the unfathomably ancient nature of the magic.

As I walked into the darkening passageway, I lost the last of the light and had to find my way by running my hands along the walls to each side. The tunnel did not branch, as far as my hands could tell, but neither did it open to the outside.

I was mightily relieved when I saw a dim light far ahead. Believing it was sunlight, or what passed for sunlight here, I quickened my pace. As I got closer, though, I could smell smoke, and I knew the light was a fire.

"Come closer," said a voice. "I won't hurt you."

I froze, estimating my odds of getting back out the way I had come in.

"It's me. It's Jude. I won't hurt you, whichever one you are. I can't after all, even if I wanted to."

The voice *sounded* like Jude.

I inched forward, not making a sound. At least I thought I wasn't.

"That's right," Jude said. "I have tea and a blanket."

"I'm not cold," I replied.

Jude cocked his head in my direction.

"Ah, Paul. It's you. Come. Come sit with me by the fire."

I walked cautiously into the little alcove where he had laid his fire, scanning for another entrance, for people lying in wait. But the roundish room was empty except for Jude. The smoke from the fire disappeared up a hole in the top of the alcove, but I couldn't see any sunlight at the top.

Jude wore a cloth of gray wool, wrapped around him like a toga. His right shoulder and his legs below the knee were uncovered. He, too, was in his original body, the Jude who had worked beside me in the Muristan in Jerusalem all those centuries ago. His exposed skin was covered in an elaborate pattern of welts, some crusting over, some running with blood or pus. His left eye was swollen around the orbit, but limp in the middle where the eyeball should be. He saw me staring at it.

"I'll grow another one back. I always do. And they'll find another creative way to pluck it out," he said, his voice flat.

"I'm sorry for your suffering," I whispered.

"You should be," Jude replied, again without inflection. "The loneliness is the worst part, though. Sometimes I get so lonely while I'm hiding that I let them find me. At least it is some human contact."

I took the folded cloth on the ground next to him, a lighter shade of gray than the one he wore and wrapped it around my body as he had. Then I sat on the cave floor across the fire from him.

"What news, then?" he asked.

"I thought you could look in whenever you wanted."

"It requires me to be still and safe, which is not easy, and when it is easy and I try to look at your world, our world, the pain is too great. It's like dying of thirst and all you can see are beautiful clear streams of cold water." He paused for a moment. "I'll understand if you don't want to talk."

We were quiet for a moment before I said, "They landed on the moon."

"The Americans or the Soviets?" he asked, sitting up.

"Americans. It was just a few years ago, but they've been more than once now. The lunar landscape is being decorated with American flags," I said.

"Always the jingoists," he said, stirring the fire.

"They're just proud, I think. Their war should be over soon," I said.

"They're *still* fighting? How many years have they been at it now? I didn't think it would last that long when you exiled me. The Nazis and the Japanese had everybody on the ropes when I left."

"The Germans surrendered," I said. "Their country is now divided between the West and the Russians."

"Soviets," he corrected.

"Soviets," I agreed.

"And Japan?"

"Big bomb," I said.

"Must have been. Did it wipe out the whole country? I can't believe they would have surrendered."

95

"Wiped out a couple of cities," I explained. "They did surrender after that."

"Hmm. So, this is a new war you're talking about?" he asked.

"There was another one in between," I said.

"I guess it's always been like that," Jude replied. "The Nazis would have put a stop to all that, you know."

"Like they put a stop to six million Jews?" I asked, raising my voice.

"The most powerful men are always excessive. Look at Genghis Khan," he said.

"You think the Khan is a point in your favor?" I asked.

"History is written by the victors," Jude said. "If Hitler had succeeded, we'd be talking about him like any of the other successful conquerors."

"You haven't changed much, brother," I began. I was suddenly lightheaded. My fingers and toes tingled, and my vision went blurry.

"Wait," he said his voice rising. "Just a little longer, *please*."

His pleading was the last thing I heard before I was born, again.

Part Four: October.

Seventeen

Frogmore, South Carolina.

I was awakened by persistent hammering on my door. The noise had a familiar quality, and since we were all at headquarters to coordinate our anti-Roosevelt efforts, I assumed it was one of the knights. I was wrong.

Joe from Penn Center was on my stoop, brandishing a newspaper, the kind made of paper, with ink and everything. He had opened his mouth and taken a breath, then seemed to register my sleepy face and bathrobe. His face and body recomposed themselves.

"St. Paul," he said, smiling and extending his hand.

You know how some people will say of a man "He's a prince"? Joe really was a prince. I never met a lord or a king with better manners.

"Coffee?" I asked retreating into Cambridge House. Joe closed the door as he followed me in.

"Love some," he said.

When we had sat down, mugs in hand, my eyes fully opened. Joe patiently passed the paper to me. He had folded it so the story he wanted me to read was on top.

COMMIE MONKS ACCUSED OF TAX FRAUD

I read it several times. I understood all the words but put together they made no sense. (1) We weren't communists; (2) We were no longer a religious order; and (3) We were a C corporation for tax purposes. An accountant audited James's work on our return every year.

Roosevelt himself had named us, the Order of St. John, as a scam organization. "They take donations, and they claim to be part of the church, but they're nothing but Godless communist spies, you can quote me on that." The paper did, indeed, quote him on that. He also said that he "wouldn't be surprised if it came to light that the Order of St. John had something to do with Prentiss Gilchrist's assassination." Always pepper the most outrageous lies with just a touch of truth. Despite the presence of thirty thousand or so cell phones, though, no picture of Aurora at Gilchrist's rally existed anywhere.

James is the best.

"He painted a target on you folks, and it's working," Joe said. "I went out to get some milk, and there's cars backed up all the way across the bridge, both bridges for that matter."

"Fuck, fuck, fuck," I muttered, tugging on some pants. "Joe, you'd better get home. We're going to have to pull up the drawbridge, and you won't be able to get out once we do. Thank you"—I stuttered for a moment, then regained control— "Thank you for everything. No, go on, and you don't know us, you don't know anything about us. You've never been here."

His eyelids fell almost closed, but I could see his pupils moving back at forth as if they were at a tennis game being played at the speed of light.

"I don't know you. I don't know anything about you. I've never been here," he repeated mechanically. I led him to the door and pointed him in the direction of the road. He shuffled away, murmuring to himself. I heard scraps as he walked away. ". . . don't know you . . . Never been here . . ."

I ran to HQ and flung open the main door. One of the stones about a meter up the arch on the right is a dummy. I touched it with my palm and the front slid away. Inside was a big red button, like the SELF-DESTRUCT button in B movies. I slammed it down, and an alarm wailed.

The others arrived in minutes, and in various states of disarray. Simon was in the worst shape, his face covered in thick cream. I must have stared at him as he ran up.

"What?" he yelled over the alarm. "I moisturize, so?"

When we were all there, Peter took a key from around his neck and fitted it into a lock next to the panic button. The alarm stopped.

"We have to raise the drawbridge," I cried, breathless. "*Now!*" I grabbed Simon's hand to my right and Augustine's to my left. The rest joined hands until we were in a rough line, our backs to headquarters. Aurora was on Augustine's right, and I heard Augustine tell her to just join her will to ours.

We began to glow, gold at first, then green, then brownish green. A forest of illusionary trees sprouted all around the compound. Behind the trees, a thick lattice of power rose from the ground to form a bowl over us. The last piece of the bowl was the path from the road into the compound.

Peter yelled, "Heave!"

We all responded, "Ho!"

It took us ten pulls to raise the spell drawbridge. This would be the strongest point in the enchantment, the natural point for a full-frontal assault from the road, and we sweat and puffed with the effort. It fell into place with a clang, as if made from iron and wood instead of will and intention.

While everyone caught their breath, I handed the newspaper to Peter.

He scanned it, then set it alight with a flame from his index finger, and, cursing, threw it to the ground. He kept cursing in Italian until it was nothing but ash. The knights looked from me to Peter for an explanation.

"This is Jude's work, that son of a syphilitic whore has doxed us," he said.

"Don't be hating on sex workers," Aurora admonished.

"Not the time," I said without turning.

"He knew we would have to hunker down now," Augustine said. "He's outmaneuvered us again. He'll probably have pictures of us circulating in case we do leave headquarters."

"Those will not be easy to get," James explained. "Not for Bart or Phil or Aurora, anyway. There may be actual physical photos of the rest of us, but the 'kids'"—he smiled at his own joke; despite their youthful bodies, Bart and Phil were centuries old— "would likely only be digital, and I already have a virus that destroys those images as soon as they appear."

"But what if someone's using antivirus software?" Simon asked.

James turned toward Simon and frowned. We all found somewhere else to look.

"Okay, alright, so I'm not a computer guy," Simon replied sulkily.

"No," Augustine said, "but you are the explosives guy. Can you rig us with perimeter mines?"

"Yes," said Simon. "Of course. Just let me get cleaned up."

"I have surveillance drones in a carport in Beaufort. I'll have them in the air patrolling by nightfall," James said. "And all of the outer cameras are up and running."

"I want the widows walk staffed at all times," Peter said. "Thomas—" he began.

"Mount the fifty caliber. Already on it, chief," Thomas replied.

A machine gun would be mounted in the four-sided porch on the roof of headquarters, the widow's walk. We would take turns up there as long as the drawbridge was up.

I hooked Aurora by the arm and moved toward Bangkok House, Augustine's home, where she had two subbasements of gear.

"We've got quartermaster duties," I said.

"How do you know that?" she asked.

"We've done this drill hundreds of times. Everyone knows their role."

"It would be nice if someone told me what *my* role is," Aurora said with real tension in her voice.

"You're right. We should put together some kind of orientation," I conceded.

"But you've never had new members, yeah," she said. "So how do you know where I should go?"

"It was Jude and me on supplies, always. We need to count all of our food, water, weapons, ammunition, armor, all of it. Then Peter and Augustine will decide how to use it."

"If you guys have done this drill so many times, you and Jude must have been pretty tight," she said, her voice going soft.

"We were brothers," I said, swatting the emotion away, "close as brothers."

Eighteen

Aurora and I stacked cases of canned fruit: peaches, pears, pineapples, and a canned salad full of uniformly cubed fruits, all some shade of yellow or orange, punctuated by maraschino cherries. They called it fruit cocktail. It was neither.

"That first summer I did not write, I stacked fruit," Aurora said from behind a tall pile of boxes.

"Always hated Thoreau," I said. "He seemed like a phony to me."

"Me, too," Aurora agreed. "And when I did the research, it seems he really was."

"Another guru gone," I replied.

"The Romantics were really full of themselves," she said.

"Quite a contrast with 'our nada, who art in nada,'" I said.

Aurora scrunched her nose.

"Also, totally full of himself," she replied, plopping herself down on a five-gallon bucket of lima beans. "I like the stories, but Papa Hemingway was such a fucking gorilla."

"He showed us in the end," I answered. "Twelve gauge to the face. Hollow be his nada."

That got a snort from her. I sat down on the bucket next to hers, and she passed me a water bottle. I took a long pull, and when I handed it back to her, she gave me a funny look.

"Why do they call them the 'Returned'?" she asked. "Where did they return from?"

I looked at my watch.

"We've got plenty of time," she chided. "We've got all of the armaments inventoried. Besides, this is part of my orientation."

I nodded. "Okay, but we have to get back to it before they ring the dinner bell. Augustine is going to ask for a progress report."

"And she's got a wild hair acrost her ass," Aurora replied.

"Where on earth did you hear that expression?"

"Maine," she said. "I was staying at this crappy hotel on assignment, and I heard a man and a woman having a big fight out by the pool—"

"Couldn't have been that crappy if they had a pool," I interrupted.

"Pool was empty, kind of a mushroom farm. *Anyway,* I step out the door of my room to see if the woman needs help just as she storms off waving both middle fingers up over her head. The guy looks at me and goes, 'She's got a wild hair acrost her ass.' I about pissed myself laughing. I asked the other nurses that night, and they said, 'Oh yeah, a wild hair, sure.' Everyone around there says it. It means someone is

105

temporarily unduly agitated or upset.' So, the Returned?"

My brain had somehow fixated on the sight of a crazily curled hair coming out of an anus.

I shook it off.

"They are the Returned, because they returned here, to our world," I explained.

"They're human like us?"

"All of the people in the Ether are *human*. They've evolved in different ways because of the difference in our worlds, but they're people. The Returned, they are *exactly* like us. They were the most powerful mages in the world before recorded history. Thaumiel was a great sorcerer and a king. He was the first one expelled. There was a group of lesser sorcerers who banded together to send him to another dimension so they wouldn't be under his thumb. They sent him to the Ether. For reasons Thomas can explain, the Ether is the easiest dimension to reach from ours."

"Couldn't he just come back?" she asked.

"Not back then. The door between our worlds was only one-way. That group of sorcerers had managed to exile their biggest adversary, but they weren't done."

"Who were they, the group what sent Thaumiel to the Ether?" Aurora asked. She was leaning forward, elbows on her knees, barely blinking.

"I wish I'd known you were so interested. I would have told you before about them," I said.

She made a rolling motion with her hand.

"They were called the Men of the Light," I explained, and she sat straight up.

"The Illuminati?" she asked, her voice squeaking.

"Yes, but not the same ones. The ones you're thinking of were a lot later. *Anyway*," I said, mimicking her earlier impatience. She threw a pencil at me, which I caught. "The Men of the Light traveled the world. They found nine more despotic users of magic and sent them all to the Ether. That's the Returned. In time, apparently, they took over the Ether, organized it into a company with themselves at the top, and made the entire population their thralls."

"When did they 'return'?" She used her fingers to make air quotes around the last word.

"We're not sure," I said. "As best we can tell, sometime after our first reincarnations. We haven't been able to get more specific than that. Augustine spent decades analyzing the historical record for evidence of their presence in this world. We know for sure they were here at the end of the eighteenth century. Beyond that, we just don't know."

"Could they have been here before you guys and you just can't find the evidence?" she asked.

"Could be, but Augustine's pretty sure they weren't. Thomas thinks there's a connection between their reappearance and Ibn Jamay's spell that made us reincarnate, but he hasn't been able to definitively say what it is."

I finished and looked at my watch. Aurora saw my gesture, tapped the watch, which she had given me, and sprung up onto her feet.

"Nice watch," she teased.

"It is indeed," I agreed, raising one corner of my mouth and one eyebrow.

"Yeah, yeah, I'm stalling," she said. "Dried fruit next?"

"I'll do the grains," I replied.

I was just finishing counting the sacks of amaranth when the dinner bell rang in the Great Hall.

"Nobody can hear that outside?" she asked nervously.

I shook my head. On the short walk from Bangkok House to the Great Hall I looked out toward the road. Two trucks were parked at the drawbridge, their lights on. Men in camouflage tee shirts, and pants wandered back and forth, never turning toward the compound. Our wards turned them away whenever one of the men turned in our direction. The dinner bell rang again, much louder this close to the hall. The camo guys did not acknowledge anything behind them as they walked back up the road.

"See?" I said gloating a little.

"That's not going to work forever," she replied.

"Forever is a very long time," I said, but a frisson of dread ran up my back, because of course she was right.

Nineteen

Simon and Andrew removed the covers on their platters with a flourish.

"*Voilà*," cried Simon.

"Coq au vin with root vegetables," Andrew said. He made a spectacle of keeping his voice calm and even.

Simon glared at him and said, "*Et voila*," and gestured toward the platters.

"I've opened a wonderful Viognier," Peter said, ignoring the other two knights. "Not an obvious pairing, I admit. But the combination will surprise you."

"*Mio signore*," Andrew said, bowing. "Should we not be avoiding this kind of excess, the food, the wine?"

Peter put his knife and fork down harder than necessary and turned to Andrew.

"You want us to start rationing on the first night?" Peter barked.

"That would be the prudent thing to do," Augustine replied under her breath.

"No," said Peter, standing. "I will not have it. Tonight, we feast. Tomorrow, we fight. That is how it has always been."

"Fight how?" Thomas asked. "We're stuck here. We don't even have a sally port. We're not going to bust through the wards, guns blazing. With all the people roaming around outside, we wouldn't get a hundred meters without an attack."

"We're not the Rat Patrol," Aurora said from the end of the table.

"You don't know anything about the Rat Patrol," Augustine said, not trying to hide her annoyance.

"Binged the whole show, both seasons, all fifty-eight episodes," Aurora responded.

Bart perked up.

"Their driver, Private Pettigrew, he had game," he said.

"The shizzle," his brother Phil agreed.

"Those guys knew how to handle a fifty cal," Thomas said, still chewing.

Peter lifted another forkful of chicken, chuckling all the while.

I enjoy a little levity as much as the next guy, but I was with Andrew on this: feasting seemed imprudent. I patted my mouth with a napkin, preparing to launch into the fray, when I looked down the table at Aurora's plate. It was heaped with food, but it wasn't showing any signs of moving toward her mouth. She was pushing it around on the plate while bantering with the others. Augustine sits next to me, and I could tell she noticed it, too. We exchanged a look but said nothing.

Simon had moved on from Rat Patrol to tell war stories about various items that he had removed from patients' rectums. It was a tough transition, but Simon knows his audience. It's little known by civilians, but all ER nurses have stuck-in-the-butt stories: flashlights, cell phones, Christmas ornaments, various fruits and vegetables. My favorite was the one about a guy who got a Barbie stuck up there. We had heard them all before, but I have to admit, they were still pretty funny. The best part was always the explanation for how the "foreign body" had made its way rectum-ward: they fell on them.

Again, civilians won't understand, but I was choking with laughter and Peter was pounding the table. Simon is a terrific mimic. He does great voices and that was a lot of what made these stories so funny.

Around the table eyes streamed with tears and faces went red. Phil claimed he peed himself "a little."

All except Andrew. Our counselor was not amused. Peter clapped him on the back, and the laughing died down to chittering.

"We fight tomorrow, Andrew, but not like the Rat Patrol," Peter said, clearing his throat. "James will be our general for this battle."

James looked embarrassed.

"Just the technical stuff. Augustine has drawn up the plan of battle," he said.

"We're going to, what, surveil them into submission?" Andrew asked, voice rising. He realized his mistake immediately. "I'm sorry, James, I meant no offense."

James looked even more embarrassed.

"S'alright," he said. "We're going to attack them on the web, in social media, chat rooms, message boards. We're going to flood the comments on a bunch of different platforms."

Andrew drew back his chair and stood. He bowed to Peter and to James.

"My sincerest apologies, brother. That is. . ." he paused and looked at the ground. When he lifted his head, his eyes were wide, and he was wearing a huge smile. "That is fucking brilliant!" he cried.

"Now we're talking," Thomas said. "We going to merge magic with the tech?"

"We are," James agreed.

"We're the troll farm for the good guys," Aurora squealed. She raised her glass, and we all drank to James.

To the age of chivalry.

To popes past and present and their orchestras.

Fuck the popes past and present.

To those who could not be with us.

To all those present.

New bottles were opened, and the round of toasts began again.

The last thing I thought as I stumbled into bed at Cambridge House was how familiar it was going to be rushing into battle with a hangover.

We assembled the next morning in the Great Hall. All except Bart who was on guard duty on the widow's walk. At each knight's place was a thirty-inch monitor, keyboard, and mouse. Cables snaked through the room and connected to little boxes behind the monitors.

Augustine leaned her head into my back.

"Kill me," she whispered.

"Huh?" I replied.

"Sorry," she said, straightening up. "The head is, well, I think I'm soon to be dead above the neck."

Best to let the straight line just lie there. (You've *always* been dead above the neck, yuck, yuck, yuck.") It would have been like arm-wrestling a child. "Did you see what I saw last night, I mean Aurora not eating?"

"I saw. We need to talk to her," I said. "I think we should do it together."

"Agreed. At the midday break."

I nodded my agreement and settled into my chair. The Order's screensaver, a black background with a 3D spinning Maltese Cross, evaporated as soon as I touched the mouse. James's face appeared on the screen. He described different assignments for each knight, some misinformation, some countertrolling the stuff from Roosevelt's team.

"Why aren't you with us?" I asked the screen. I assumed he could hear me, but I was embarrassed that perhaps I had been speaking to an inanimate object.

"You're on mute," Augustine said reaching over to click something with my mouse. I nodded thanks.

"WHY AREN'T YOU WITH US?" I shouted.

On the screen, James pulled his earphones away from his ears, much to my chagrin and the general amusement of the others at the table.

"I'm at Nairobi House. The servers are all here, and I'm putting the magic into them."

"Ah," I replied, having no idea what he was saying.

My assignment matched my abilities with technology, which is to say, silly, undignified, and limited. I was given a doctored photo of Garridan Roosevelt in drag. He had a gigantic pink wig on, a peignoir, and Dr. Frank-N-Furter stockings.

"First, who cares if he wants to wear clothes that make him feel pretty? How is this going to hurt him?" I asked.

"It's no big deal to you and me," said Simon, "but to his people this will be like eating babies."

"Surely they aren't *that* ignorant," I responded.

"First, don't call me Shirley," said Simon patiently. "Second, you really don't get the enemy. My dear Paul, they are vicious, and they are dumb. There are a sizable number of Roosevelt supporters who believe the earth is flat."

"No," Bart sputtered, "you're making that up."

Simon handed his phone to Bart who flipped through some screens.

"Christ almighty," Bart whispered. "How can this be?"

"This is mostly the Returned's doing," Andrew explained, "but they've tapped into something ugly, too, and now it's taken on a life of its own."

"Believing the world was flat, that was for peasants who never left their villages, who knew nothing but their tiny world. How could people believe this in a world where everyone reads, where everyone has access to centuries of knowledge on the web?" Bart asked. His shoulders slumped. "Have we lost already?"

"The battle is young," Peter said from the head of the table.

"Let's fuck these idiots up," Aurora called from the other end. We pounded the table a few times in agreement. Then I started posting pictures of Drag Garridan Roosevelt, and you know, he made a hell of a good-looking drag queen. If he hadn't been so homophobic, the picture might have been something he was proud of.

Twenty

One week before the election. Frogmore, South Carolina.

Augustine had just thrashed me, *again*, at Boggle. Thomas bounced a rubber ball over and over against the brick chimney, and the smell of baking bread wafted in from the kitchen.

"Simon's making more sourdough?" I asked, shaking the Boggle letters again.

"I've put eighteen loaves in the freezer, so far," Augustine replied.

"Yahtzee!" Aurora yelled from the kitchen, where she and Bart and Phil were rolling dice.

Philip growled, and Bart said, "There's no way that was natural. You charmed it. Admit it."

"Did you feel any magic?" Aurora asked. I recognized that tone of voice. She was baiting them.

"No," Bart admitted. "Doesn't mean there wasn't any."

This was followed by a satisfied "Hmmpf" from my daughter and the rattling of dice in a cup.

James knocked on the doorframe as he came in.

"You guys should see this," he said, opening his computer. The dice rolling stopped and the Yahtzee contestants emerged followed by Simon wearing an apron and covered in flour. James flicked his fingers at the computer and his screen was projected on the wall.

"These are from the last three nights," he said.

The videos were night-lit in that eerie green that night vision lenses put on everything. The first image, from three nights ago, showed a group of people, all men, as far as we could tell, shambling like cartoon villains, sneaking.

If you're going to hunt the wabbit, be vewy, vewy quiet.

They walked right up to the wards and did not turn away. One of them looked at his watch, which glowed bright white in the night vision camera.

"That's the enchantment," Thomas said, not taking his eyes from the screen. "That watch is showing them our boundaries."

The camouflaged men assembled along the edge of the wards. The men farthest from the guy with the watch shook and fell, convulsing on the ground. Reactions increased with distance from the watch. Watch Guy nodded to himself and tilted his head away from our boundary. They walked about twenty meters back into the woods, then Watch Guy threw a stick that hit the wards and lit up before falling to the ground.

"Not good," said Thomas, "not good at all. The illusions are failing."

"Can they get through *your* wards?" Augustine asked. Thomas is our best with magic. While we can all create wards, nobody comes close to Thomas's power.

"They aren't just *my* wards. We all put power into them," Thomas said.

"You directed it. You wove the spell," Augustine countered.

"No wards are impenetrable," he replied. "And with Thaumiel in our plane, they have plenty of power to bring to the fight."

"That's not scary at all," Simon muttered.

"Sir Simon Zealotes," Augustine spat, standing, "I have seen you rush headlong into cannon fire. Why are you behaving like this?"

"I've got so much more bread to bake," he said.

"Don't be an ass," Augustine said, sitting back down.

James shushed us and hit play on the video from two nights ago.

The guy with the watch was back at the same spot, but this time, two other guys with watches appeared on other cameras. They all repeated Watch Guy's moves from the night before, complete with thrown stick. The groups were arranged three-quarters of the way around our magical defenses; no one was in front of the drawbridge. In fact, the road leading to the drawbridge was empty. To the average passerby, it looked like the road ended with a concrete barrier. Their formation, though, showed us that they knew where the drawbridge was.

This night, however, the groups had walkie-talkies and headsets. The three watch guys mumbled into their microphones, then simultaneously drew silenced AR15's and fired shots at the wards. Every bullet strike lit up the barrier and caused ripples in the wards, like stones thrown into a deep pond.

We were quiet when James paused the video.

"They know where our defenses are, and they know that small arms fire won't penetrate them. Even a tank couldn't get through them without magical energy," Augustine said. She hesitated, eyes moving back and forth. "I think I know what's coming," she said. "Show us last night."

James started the video. All of the cameras were clear and empty until the camera facing the road showed a blurry dark figure.

"Can you make that clearer?" Augustine asked.

"No," James replied with a finality that made the room even more tense.

In front of the blurry figure flashes and ripples showed all over the drawbridge. I realized all at once that they were shots, and they were outlining the strongest part of our defenses.

"Why didn't we see them from the widow's walk?" Phil asked, his voice hardening. "Who was on watch last night?"

"I was," Thomas answered. "I never saw a thing."

"I was on the night before," added Simon. "Ditto."

"The night before that, it was me," Augustine said, although she was only half paying attention. Her brain was working on a plan. "Do we still have the tunnel under Amalfi House?"

"We do," Simon replied. "It's not open at the far end, but I could do that."

"Not yet," Augustine said. "How far beyond the wards does it come out?"

"Thirty meters," Simon said.

"We don't want to open it yet," Augustine began. "If we do, and they keep poking, they will find it and have an easy way in."

"I'll extend the wards into the tunnel," Thomas replied.

"That will help some," Augustine said. "It won't much though if they find the tunnel. We'll have to keep a close eye on that stretch of the perimeter. Can we make frequent flybys with the drones?"

"You should see the last part of the video first," James said, and tapped play.

The camera showed a moving gray image against a darker gray sky.

"They look like UFO's," Bart said.

The screen was divided into views from six different cameras. All six screens lit up, then showed the drones exploding, pieces crashing in different directions.

"Shotguns," I said, "like shooting geese."

"Had to be pretty powerful shotguns," Augustine countered. "Those drones were fifty meters up. We should hold all of our gatherings in Amalfi House from now on. That way we'll have access to the tunnel at all times if we need it. Aurora, tell Peter to expect us."

"He was up all night working on the social media campaign with Andrew, who, by the way, is amazing at trolling," Aurora replied.

"Peter will understand," Augustine said, "and of course Andrew is good at mind games. That's his specialty. Everyone packs a bag and moves to Peter's. Paul and Aurora, set up an armory in the tunnel. Assault weapons only. We'll use small arms and not melee weapons if we have to fight our way out."

"A sword never runs out of ammunition," I said.

"And it's only good a meter away from you. If they come for us it will mean they have a plan, that the *Returned* have a plan. I can't imagine they will take the time to get close. I wouldn't. In any event, I don't expect them to make a move until after the election. It's clear we're not having much of an impact on their poll numbers so far. They'll have plenty of time to deal with us once the election's over."

Aurora ran to me, phone in hand, her face in panic.

"Miranda just arrived in Charleston. She wants to watch the election results with us. She flew in to surprise me."

Twenty-One

Augustine, Aurora, and I sat in a semicircle facing the big computer screen in the Great Hall. If Peter had known we were here, he would have been angry. We were directly disobeying orders to stay at Amalfi, but this had to be done, and we wanted to respect Aurora's privacy.

Miranda's face appeared on the screen, wide-eyed and big-grinned. She looked right at Aurora, beaming, but as she took in the two of us sitting next to Aurora, her brow knitted.

"Hey, sweetie," she said, fidgeting with excitement. "What's going on?"

"Hello, my love," Aurora replied with a look both pregnant and complex. "It is so incredibly sweet that you came all this way to be with me. I didn't expect to see you until my next assignment. How's your mom and dad? Your brother?"

"Good," Miranda said, warily. "When will you be here to pick me up? I just got my suitcase from the checked baggage thingy. I can't wait to see you."

"That's the thing," I interrupted. "It's not safe for you here right now."

Miranda's face contracted in alarm.

"Headquarters is locked down, dear," Augustine said. "There's no safe way in or out."

"Locked down? Why?" Miranda looked to each of us.

"The bad guys have found us," Aurora said. "And this time it's some *really* bad guys."

"You can't stay in there forever," Miranda said.

"I know," said Aurora. She was wringing her hands under the table. "But we think we'll have a better chance after the election. They're keeping us contained to improve Roosevelt's chances."

"Roosevelt is one of them, for sure?"

"Oh yeah," I said. "The baddest of the bad."

"Fuckers," Miranda said. Her face turned into a pout for just a second, then it was gone. "What can I do to help?"

The three of us at headquarters all started talking at once. Augustine and I stopped.

"Excuse us," Augustine said, abashed.

Aurora waved it away.

"You have to get back home. You have to keep your head down," Aurora said. "They must know of our relationship, and that will put you in danger."

"They must know where I live," said Miranda. Her hands went to her mouth. "My family," she cried.

"I sent them an encrypted message with instructions. We have a safe house for them in California," I said. "Will they know what to do with it?"

"My father's an IT engineer. What do you think?" Miranda said sharply. "I'm sorry, Paul. It's not your fault." She looked at Aurora appraisingly. "How do you deal with this *all the time*?"

"Part of the job," she replied, and the sincerity meter didn't register at all. "We all have our ways of coping."

"You haven't been eating," Miranda answered. It wasn't a question, just a bald statement of fact. "I can always tell. Angel, talk to me."

Aurora cut her eyes at us. I coughed and excused myself, pulling Augustine behind me.

"We should have made sure Miranda was behind the wards before we pulled up the drawbridge," Augustine said once we were outside. "She's family, after all."

I nodded, and I felt the weight of the world on my shoulders. My daughter's future, her happiness, maybe her sanity, all depended on how we handled the next few minutes.

"There wasn't any time. If Joe hadn't brought the paper, we might not have gotten the defenses up in time," I said. "Weird to think that a printed newspaper was what kept us safe."

"It *is* weird," she agreed. "James has bots all over the web constantly looking for information about us. He should have seen it hours before the newspaper came out. We'll need to talk to him about it when we get back to Amalfi House. In the meantime, I found an ally who will take Miranda to a private jet. The owner used to be in the Left Hand of God, and I was worried she wouldn't help us, but she said she can take Miranda to the safe house in California."

"And you trust her? I don't want to take any chances with my, um, daughter-in-law," I said. Man, did that sound odd. "Are you sure this ally isn't working for the enemy somehow?"

"There are no sure things," Augustine replied. "I checked her out, and James checked her out, and Thomas did a finding. That's the best we can do."

A finding is when a sorcerer scans the environment for traces of dark magic, magical footprints. With the help of technology, Thomas can project his senses to almost any physical location on earth, but not *every* location at once. Augustine would have pointed him to the places where this ally had been over the last six months.

"I don't like the idea of taking any chances with Miranda," I said. "This is Aurora's first lifetime. What happens here will be with her for a long time, and I don't want her to have to bear the heartbreak you did."

"Nor do I," Augustine said. "That was hundreds of years ago, but you're right; it still haunts me. The loss of Gerald was—" She paused and collected herself. "But it wasn't at the hands of the Returned. If we lose Miranda, who knows how that could change Aurora?"

"A knight bent solely on revenge would be hard to manage," I agreed.

"Aurora's heartbreak would be horrible for all of us, Paul. You're not the only one who loves her. You're not the only one who loves Miranda, for that matter."

I slipped my hand around the back of Augustine's neck and pulled our foreheads together, and we stood like that in silence for a moment.

"You're kind of her mom," I said when we separated.

"Don't be ridiculous," she replied, but the corners of her mouth curved, and her eyes narrowed, and I knew her well enough to know this was how she expressed delight. "We need to talk to her about the anorexia, right away. She's probably further down the rabbit hole than we know."

Augustine didn't say it, because she really loved Aurora, but as our general, she had to be thinking it: we also needed Aurora for the fight that was coming.

Augustine knocked on the door to the Great Hall, and, after a moment, Aurora answered, "Come in."

She was wiping away tears, and Miranda's bigger-than-life face on the screen was doing the same.

"We have a plan," Aurora announced. "Miranda is going back to California. I am going to have dinner. Then I want you"—I pointed to my own chest, and Aurora shook her head— "you, Augustine, to help

126

me prepare for what's coming. I'm really scared, and I won't hide any of it from you anymore."

That didn't sound ominous.

Augustine pulled her into a hug. When it was over, she looked at the screen.

"Take your bags right now and go to a stairway on the east side of the building. It's mostly used by the housekeepers. Go to the bottom of the stairs. It comes out next to a loading dock, not on the ground floor. There's a car waiting right now. It will flash its lights four times. Get in the back seat and don't say anything. The driver is not to speak with you. If he or she says anything, text us right away. The driver will take you to a plane that will fly you to the safe house where your parents are staying. Any questions?"

Miranda shook her head.

"Go now," Augustine said, "and good luck."

Twenty-Two

The Knight-Nurses of the Order of St. John sat on or draped themselves over various pieces of furniture on a Sunday morning. An urn of coffee was right at home on the coffee table, next to the remains of a pyramid of mugs. The mugs were flanked by a quart of half-and-half and a sugar bowl. Peter had made two panettones, one with cranberries and chocolate, the other with just candied fruit. Both were crumbs on a platter now.

I had eaten my share and was on my third cup of coffee when the first of the morning talking head shows started, *Meet the Nation*. The second show, on a different network, *Face the Press*, started an hour later. Jude was going to be on both of them, the campaign manager making his case two days before the election. Garridan Roosevelt had retired to his tent, which, in this case, was a villa on Lake Huron.

Usually when we watched a show like this, we behaved like peasants at the gladiatorial games, much shouting, cursing, and inappropriate comments, by which I mean all manner of sexual innuendo. Not so this morning.

My brothers and sisters were seldom this quiet. It reminded me of chapel in the old days. After the sports-like graphics, swelling music, and dramatic close-up of the moderator, I was impressed by the lack of gravity in the interview. Modern Americans must be entertained at all times.

We were watching bread and circus more than sixteen hundred years after the fall of the Roman empire. *Nihil sub sole novum.* I'm not a bible guy anymore—once, a long time ago—but watching the opening to *Meet the Nation*, one of my favorite bible passages came to mind. This one from Ecclesiastes:

Vanity of vanities, everything is vanity.

What advantage does man get from all the hardships that come under the sun?

One generation goes, another comes, and the earth never changes.

The sun rises, the sun sets; and soon returns to its place to go out again.

The wind blows to the south and turns to the north; then it spins again, and it doesn't stop spinning.

All rivers go to the sea, and the sea is never full; and the rivers return to their origin to travel the same path.

There is no one capable of expressing how boring things are; no one sees or hears enough to be satisfied.

What has happened happens again; and what has been done before is what will be done. There is nothing new under the sun.

If there is someone who says: This is something new! This already existed centuries before us.

I'm a little burned-out after nine hundred years. Does it show?

If this is Aurora's world, not mine, why does it feel exactly the same? The technical marvels of the twenty-first century haven't done much to improve the basic goodness of humanity. I'm not willing to say that technology is to blame. Peter says it often enough for all of us. But when I watch the opening to a show whose purpose is allegedly to help the electorate make sense of the policy differences between candidates, all I see is farmers in homespun eating peanuts and cheering for their champion to cut the other guy's head off.

I have to admit, though, Jude looks sharp. He hasn't been good-looking in all of his incarnations, but he has been a good dresser. This isn't an incarnation, strictly speaking, because he's occupying somebody else's body. Nonetheless, he cuts a sophisticated and charming figure. So why are the farmers with peanuts rooting for him? I have no earthly idea, as my wife used to say. This was back in Manchester, England, eighteen eighties, long story. I have seen few politicians in my lives who look *less* like "the people" than Garridan Roosevelt, and Jude is right on brand.

He banters with the host, who is not overtly hostile to him, but Jude has correctly guessed that the host is not a Roosevelt supporter. After the initial scuffles, all of Jude's answers to the reporters' questions are canned talking points. Try as they may, they cannot get him off script.

Just when I think I'm too bored to keep watching. He turns toward the camera and looks directly at me.

"Keeping you up, Paul?" he asks.

"I guess I know why you're doing this," I replied. "I just thought you were tougher than that. I thought you would do your time like a man. And to be honest, I didn't think it was possible to slip the chains we put you in."

"Brother Paul," Jude intoned, closing his eyes and putting his hands together. "My self-righteous friend. The corporation is more powerful than you can imagine. There's still time to join us. We can use someone with your talents in the New World." The other knights were frozen in place.

"You are making them the same offers?" I asked.

"Most of them," he replied. "Peter and Augustine can go fuck themselves and Doubting Thomas may be too much for us to handle, but the rest. You know one of them is going to come to our side. Spare yourself the coming pain."

"What about Aurora?" I growled. "If you hurt her in any way, I swear I will not rest until—"

His deep laugh cut me off.

"My"—he snickered— "replacement? You want to keep her from talking to *me*? I forget sometimes, Paul, how thick you are with sentimentality. You can't see what's right in front of you."

131

"What's right in front of me?"

"The cuckoo, of course," he said, and chuckled again.

"What's that supposed to mean?" My muscles tensed, readying for a fight, but my guts went the other direction.

"I can see your little mind furiously working, brother. The cuckoo puts her egg in another bird's nest, see. The other bird hatches the egg and raises the chick," Jude said, and his pleasure in saying it was unbearable.

"You. Are. A. Liar." I spat.

"I am many things, Paul, but not a liar. Betrayal is a kind of lie, I guess. But you know in your heart I'm not lying. And what matters to Paul more than his heart? Hmm? She's ours, Paul. She belongs to us."

"*Bullshit!*" I screamed. My right arm became pure energy. I reached into the screen, toward Jude's throat. The screen died in a flurry of white sparks. When I withdrew my arm, it was burned from the fingertips to the elbow.

As soon as the screen died the others started moving. Peter's curses were so laced with anger that what was left of the screen melted into slag.

"That was really expensive," said James, shaking his head at the plastic puddle on the floor.

"What did he promise you?" I asked, turning to James.

"The usual," James replied. "Thirty pieces of silver or the modern equivalent. Same Jude, different day."

Bart and Phil exchanged glances.

"He said we could run NASA," Phil said, blinking. "The Returned have a method for space travel unknown here."

"He knows where to hit," Bart agreed. "I hate that motherfucker so much."

Andrew chewed his lip.

"His temptation for me wasn't astute. It tells me that he's so turned inward on himself that he may have some blind spots that we can exploit," he said.

"I'm listening," said Thomas.

"He was offering to make me their Joseph Goebbels, the head of propaganda," Andrew said.

"You'd be scary good at that job," I muttered.

Andrew waved the compliment away.

"Maybe," he said, "but I'd never do it. I'd spend eternity in the Ether first. Jude knows that about me, but he's projecting his obsession with power on us. We can use that."

"He *offered* me an eternity in the Ether," Thomas scoffed. "He said they couldn't have me running around loose."

Augustine sat, tapping her lips with her index finger.

"He gave me a detailed description of how they're going to torture me," she said. "I'm guessing he did the same to Peter."

Peter was still too angry to speak.

At the far end of the room, Aurora was closed into a ball, her head between her knees, hands over her head. I went to her and sat on the floor next to her. I stroked her hair and told her to breathe. Her only response was to push her head deeper between her knees.

Augustine appeared on the other side of her.

"What did he say to you?" Augustine asked. Aurora groaned in such misery, she sounded like a dying animal. It was deep, raw pain turned into sound. "Darling," Augustine said, her voice soft and tender. "What did he say?"

She made that hideous, lonely sound again, then through stuttering breaths she said, "He said 'welcome home.'"

Twenty-Three

Election Night Part Two, Frogmore, South Carolina

We fled the enveloping maelstrom. Each of us creating a shield that could protect us until we were down in the tunnel under Amalfi House. The election had been called for Roosevelt, and within minutes his minions were attacking our headquarters. At least one of the Returned must have been with them, because serious magic had been brought to bear against our wards.

I was not the last one down the ladder and into the tunnel. Thomas and Aurora were behind me, back in the inferno. Although I expected they were using magic to keep from being burned alive, they were cut off from access to the tunnel. The smart thing to do would have been to seal the entrance so that nothing could follow me down the tunnel. That meant abandoning the knights behind me, my daughter included, to their fate.

"A nonstarter," as they say in the Ether.

I gathered my thoughts, my will, my love for Aurora and Thomas and lifted the flaming river away from the hole in Peter's floor. The

135

weight of the flames got heavier as I climbed the steps, raising it like a carpet from below. By the time I got to the top step, my arms were shaking. Three deep thuds nearby, no doubt artillery shells, had my legs shaking, too, with the vibrations from the impact.

The smoke and heat and dizzying strain made it almost impossible to see, as I turned in a circle looking for my daughter and my brother. Thomas was fighting hand to hand with two men in black body armor, the three of them encased in a clear bubble around which the flames flowed like water. Thomas dropped one of them to the floor with a hand strike to the throat. The other armored man hit Thomas with a haymaker from behind, throwing him forward against the wall of the bubble. The soldier still standing reached for his sidearm, but before he even touched the grip, a lance of white light severed his arm neatly between the wrist and elbow. Then his head tilted back with the impact from a Louisville Slugger, and Aurora helped Thomas to his feet.

She had remembered to grab my bat.

Aurora and Thomas saw me at the same time, my arms slowly lowering, the river of fire closer and closer to my head, and they began running. The magical bubble around them rolled like a hamster ball. As it reached me, Thomas took the weight of the fire with one hand—always showing off—while I backed down the stairs. Thomas backed down after me, Aurora watching his back. I had reached the bottom of the stairs, and Aurora was just stepping down through the hatch, when fire pushed through her shield.

Long fingers of flame reached in and grabbed Aurora around the waist. She screamed, and Thomas locked his free hand onto one of her ankles. I lunged up the stairs and grabbed the other ankle, but whatever was pulling against us was insanely strong. It shook Thomas and me like a dog with a toy, and when we finally went flying in opposite directions Aurora was drawn upward, and the floor slammed shut, cutting off Aurora's wailing scream.

I sprang at the tunnel door, pushing, pumping power into the weight of it. I looked for some kind of electronics to open it. When nothing worked, I banged my fists against it, my flesh sizzling and blistering with each blow. Thomas was saying something I couldn't hear. I don't know if it was the buzzing in my head or the roar of the fire above that drowned him out, but I heard nothing.

Then I was asleep, which is a dirty trick to play on a brother.

I awoke running at a full sprint, Thomas's hand on the back of my head. I ducked, dislodging his hand, and spun toward him, my body glowing.

"Paul, *stop*," he cried, stepping back. "We can't save her if you kill me."

My glow weakened.

"We need to get to the others and regroup," he said, but his voice still rang with panic.

"No, no, no, no, no," I murmured. "I'm not going to leave her there."

"We all love her," Thomas said, tension bleeding from his stance. "None of us would leave her behind. If you were thinking rationally, you would know that."

"I can't think rationally," I growled. "My daughter has been taken by magical fire."

"I was there," Thomas shot back. "I think I know what it was, but we'll need Simon to defeat it."

"Galachab."

"I don't think any of them can work fire like he can," Thomas replied. "Simon is our best when it comes to fire. We need him. I could barely keep from being roasted back there."

I said nothing but turned and ran off down the tunnel, Thomas on my heels. The dimly lit path sloped downward. Simon had built it deeper and deeper once it crossed the wards so that it would be harder to detect. Thomas caught me up and grabbed my shoulder.

"The tunnel is supposed to be collapsing behind us," he said.

"It's waiting for Aurora," I said. "Knowing Simon, it won't fall until we're all through."

Thomas considered this for a moment before turning back the way we had come. He extended his arms to either side, then clapped them loudly together. A wave of earth approached us.

"Now, earth magic I can do," he said, and seeing the anxiety on my face added, "It won't bury us. It will close behind us. Let's go."

A few moments later—thirty seconds? Three weeks? Who knows

at a time like that? —we cleared a bend, and the rest of the knights were waiting for us. Augustine ran past me to the approaching earthen wall.

"Where is she? What happened? How could you leave her?" Augustine screamed, and I wrapped my arms around her.

"Simon," Thomas cried, ignoring Augustine, "Galachab has her." Simon's eyes became flickers of flame. The tunnel opened above us, a starry night peaking down into our little den. Simon said nothing. He leaped and was borne upward as he dissolved into a cloud of fire.

"I'm going with him," Augustine yelled, vaulting to the top of the tunnel. She began firing as soon as her feet hit the ground. I jumped up, and we stood back-to-back, a magical shield in front of each of us. Our rifle barrels took on a dull red from all the rounds. There were so many bullets hitting my shield that I watched wrinkles forming on the back of my hand. Each act of magic costs us time, depletes our lives. The magical energy required to maintain my shield would kill me if I kept it up for too long.

To my right mature hardwood trees snapped like summer grass under a boot. James and Peter were beside us now, reinforcing the shields. I couldn't see where all the bullets were coming from, so I was shooting blindly. I had no magical energy to enhance my vision; all of my power was concentrated on the shield. Whatever was mowing down the trees, though, wouldn't even slow down for our magic. This would be our finish, but I would die fighting, fighting to get my daughter back.

Then I remembered: Bart and Phil. They had a tank. I didn't think they had time to get to it, and in my worry about Aurora, I hadn't even noticed them missing. The tank announced itself by firing two shells ahead of Augustine's position. Ordnance pinged off the tank's armor, and the big guns swiveled and fired again in that direction. I was momentarily blinded by the light of the tank's machine gun firing to my right. A line of men appeared as they died. They had been magically cloaked. I don't know how the twins saw them, but I was glad that they had. Those invisible soldiers would have been on us in seconds.

The rain of bullets against our shields had slowed to a trickle when Andrew yelled, "Incoming." A mortar round arced toward us, already descending. If it was a magical round, our shields couldn't stop it. A comet closed on the mortar from behind, and it exploded high in the sky. The comet then floated to earth, shooting gouts of flame in every direction.

Soldiers screamed. In the distance engines roared away.

I ran to Simon. The ground around him smoldered. He was middle-aged now, probably in his forties. His hair had streaks of gray.

"She's gone," he said. "I don't know if they took her to the Ether or they've got her stashed somewhere in our world. I tried to track him, but he was already gone." Fat tears flowed down his cheeks as he lay in the ash. "I wasn't fast enough," he said before he broke into choking sobs.

140

The others arrived, riding on the tank. I helped Simon up. My blistered hands complained when they touched his too-hot flesh. It reminded me that this wasn't the only fire I had touched that night.

"We must move quickly," Peter said, "while they are in retreat. Augustine has Zodiacs for us on the north side of the island. There is a boat waiting farther off the coast. Thomas can do a finding, and we can see if she is still here on this plane."

"Garridan's president," I said. "It's probably too late for all of us."

"That's the spirit," Augustine mumbled. "Bart, get us to the coast." She rapped on the tank's lid, and it spun toward the ocean, toward our retreat.

Dear Readers,

Thanks for spending some time with me and the Council of the Order of St. John. As you can probably guess, this isn't the end of the adventure for the K-Nurses. The amazing Phil Thron narrated the audiobook for _The Road to Damascus,_ which takes the story to a whole new level.

I truly appreciate you taking the time to read my work, even if it wasn't for you. In that vein, I'd like to ask a favor. Whatever you thought of the book, good or bad, I will be in your debt if you could leave a review on Amazon.com or Goodreads.com.

Every review helps to establish the book's place in the literary world and makes it possible to keep the series going.

I hope it gives the general public some insight into the tremendous challenges nurses face today. Everyone says nurses are heroes, but that sentiment has become hollow and a poor excuse for the kind of support nurses really need. They give of themselves even when they are discouraged and burned out. If this book gives you a little peek into their world, so much the better.

Thanks for reading and all my best wishes,

Mark Leo Tapper

Other K-Nurse books available from Amazon.com:

M. L. Tapper is the Award-Winning author of *The Vials of Our Wrath*. He lives, works as a nurse, and writes speculative fiction from the home he shares with his wife Susannah, stepsons Arthur and Felix, and several STET pets, in Vermont.

You can find out more about the author and his books at MarkLeoTapper.com. Sign up at the website to receive news of events, new K-Nurse releases, and download deals.

The Road to Damascus, narrated by Phil Thron, is available from Audible.com.